THE
COUNT'S MILLIONS

HE SNATCHED UP A HEAVY BRONZE CANDELABRUM, AND BRANDISHED IT IN THE AIR, CRYING: "THE FIRST WHO APPROACHES IS A DEAD MAN!"

THE
COUNT'S
MILLIONS

Translated from the French of
EMILE GABORIAU

Illustrated by
JOHN SLOAN

Charles Scribner's Sons

New York 1913

COPYRIGHT, 1913, BY
CHARLES SCRIBNER'S SONS

ILLUSTRATIONS

THE COUNT'S MILLIONS

PASCAL AND MARGUERITE.

I.

It was a Thursday evening, the fifteenth of October; and although only half-past six o'clock, it had been dark for some time already. The weather was cold, and the sky was as black as ink, while the wind blew tempestuously, and the rain fell in torrents.

The servants at the Hôtel de Chalusse, one of the most magnificent mansions in the Rue de Courcelles in Paris, were assembled in the porter's lodge, a little building comprising a couple of rooms standing on the right hand side of the great gateway. Here, as in all large mansions, the "concierge" or porter, M. Bourigeau, was a person of immense importance, always able and disposed to make any one who was inclined to doubt his authority, feel it in cruel fashion. As could be easily seen, he held all the other servants in his power. He could let them absent themselves without leave, if he chose, and conceal all returns late at night after the closing of public balls and wine-shops. Thus, it is needless to say that M. Bourigeau and his wife were treated by their fellow-servants with the most servile adulation.

The owner of the house was not at home that evening, so that M. Casimir, the count's head valet, was serving coffee for the benefit of all the retainers. And while the company sipped the fragrant beverage which had been generously tinctured with cognac, provided by the butler, they all united in abusing their common enemy, the master of the house. For the time being, a pert little waiting-maid, with an odious turn-up nose, had the floor. She was addressing her remarks to a big, burly, and rather insolent-looking fellow, who had been added only the evening before to the corps of footmen. "The place is really intolerable," she was saying. "The wages are high, the food of the very best, the livery just such as would show off a good-looking man to the best advantage, and Madame Léon, the housekeeper, who has entire charge of everything, is not too lynx-eyed."

"And the work?"

"A mere nothing. Think, there are eighteen of us to serve only two persons, the count and Mademoiselle Marguerite. But then there is never any pleasure, never any amusement here."

"What! is one bored then?"

"Bored to death. This grand house is worse than a tomb. No receptions, no dinners—nothing. Would you believe it, I have never seen the reception-rooms! They are always closed; and the furniture is dropping to pieces under its coverings. There are not three visitors in the course of a month."

She was evidently incensed, and the new footman seemed to share her indignation. "Why, how is it?" he exclaimed. "Is the count an owl? A man who's not yet fifty years old, and who's said to be worth several millions."

"Yes, millions; you may safely say it—and perhaps ten, perhaps twenty millions too."

"Then all the more reason why there should be

something going on here. What does he do with himself alone, all the blessed day?"

"Nothing. He reads in the library, or wanders about
the garden. Sometimes, in the evening, he drives with
Mademoiselle Marguerite to the Bois de Boulogne in
a closed carriage; but that seldom happens. Besides,
there is no such thing as teasing the poor man. I've
been in the house for six months, and I've never heard
him say anything but: ' yes '; ' no '; ' do this '; ' very
well '; ' retire.' You would think these are the only
words he knows. Ask M. Casimir if I'm not right."

" Our guv'nor isn't very gay, that's a fact," re-
sponded the valet.

The footman was listening with a serious air, as if
greatly interested in the character of the people whom
he was to serve. " And mademoiselle," he asked, " what
does she say to such an existence? "

" Bless me! during the six months she has been here,
she has never once complained."

" If she is bored," added M. Casimir, " she conceals
it bravely."

" Naturally enough," sneered the waiting-maid, with
an ironical gesture; " each month that mademoiselle
remains here, brings her too much money for her to
complain."

By the laugh that greeted this reply, and by the looks
the older servants exchanged, the new-comer must have
realized that he had discovered the secret skeleton hid-
den in every house. " What! what! " he exclaimed,
on fire with curiosity; " is there really anything in that?
To tell the truth, I was inclined to doubt it."

His companions were evidently about to tell him all
they knew, or rather all they thought they knew, when
the front-door bell rang vigorously.

"There he comes!" exclaimed the concierge; "but he's in too much of a hurry; he'll have to wait awhile."

He sullenly pulled the cord, however; the heavy door swayed on its hinges, and a cab-driver, breathless and hatless, burst into the room, crying, "Help! help!"

The servants sprang to their feet.

"Make haste!" continued the driver. "I was bringing a gentleman here—you must know him. He's outside, in my vehicle——"

Without pausing to listen any longer, the servants rushed out, and the driver's incoherent explanation at once became intelligible. At the bottom of the cab, a roomy four-wheeler, a man was lying all of a heap, speechless and motionless. He must have fallen forward, face downward, and owing to the jolting of the vehicle his head had slipped under the front seat.

"Poor devil!" muttered M. Casimir, "he must have had a stroke of apoplexy." The valet was peering into the vehicle as he spoke, and his comrades were approaching, when suddenly he drew back, uttering a cry of horror. "Ah, my God! it is the count!"

Whenever there is an accident in Paris, a throng of inquisitive spectators seems to spring up from the very pavement, and indeed more than fifty persons had already congregated round about the vehicle. This circumstance restored M. Casimir's composure; or, at least, some portion of it. "You must drive into the courtyard," he said, addressing the cabman. "M. Bourigeau, open the gate, if you please." And then, turning to another servant, he added:

"And you must make haste and fetch a physician— no matter who. Run to the nearest doctor, and don't return until you bring one with you."

The concierge had opened the gate, but the driver had disappeared; they called him, and on receiving no reply the valet seized the reins and skilfully guided the cab through the gateway.

Having escaped the scrutiny of the crowd, it now remained to remove the count from the vehicle, and this was a difficult task, on account of the singular position of his body; still, they succeeded at last, by opening both doors of the cab, the three strongest men uniting in their efforts. Then they placed him in a large armchair, carried him to his own room, and speedily had him undressed and in bed.

He had so far given no sign of life; and as he lay there with his head weighing heavily on the pillow, you might have thought that all was over. His most intimate friend would scarcely have recognized him. His features were swollen and discolored; his eyes were closed, and a dark purple circle, looking almost like a terrible bruise, extended round them. A spasm had twisted his lips, and his distorted mouth, which was drawn on one side and hung half open, imparted a most sinister expression to his face. In spite of every precaution, he had been wounded as he was removed from the cab. His forehead had been grazed by a piece of iron, and a tiny stream of blood was trickling down upon his face. However, he still breathed; and by listening attentively, one could distinguish a faint rattling in his throat.

The servants, who had been so garrulous a few moments before, were silent now. They lingered in the room, exchanging glances of mute consternation. Their faces were pale and sad, and there were tears in the eyes of some of them. What was passing in their minds? Perhaps they were overcome by that uncon-

querable fear which sudden and unexpected death always provokes. Perhaps they unconsciously loved this
master, whose bread they ate. Perhaps their grief was
only selfishness, and they were merely wondering what
would become of them, where they should find another
situation, and if it would prove a good one. Not knowing what to do, they talked together in subdued voices,
each suggesting some remedy he had heard spoken of
for such cases. The more sensible among them were
proposing to go and inform mademoiselle or Madame
Léon, whose rooms were on the floor above, when the
rustling of a skirt against the door suddenly made them
turn. The person whom they called " mademoiselle "
was standing on the threshold.

Mademoiselle Marguerite was a beautiful young girl,
about twenty years of age. She was a brunette of
medium height, with big gloomy eyes shaded by thick
eyebrows. Heavy masses of jet-black hair wreathed
her lofty but rather sad and thoughtful forehead. There
was something peculiar in her face—an expression of
concentrated suffering, and a sort of proud resignation,
mingled with timidity.

" What has happened? " she asked, gently. " What
is the cause of all the noise I have heard? I have rung
three times and the bell was not answered."

No one ventured to reply, and in her surprise she
cast a hasty glance around. From where she stood, she
could not see the bed stationed in an alcove; but she
instantly noted the dejected attitude of the servants, the
clothing scattered about the floor, and the disorder that
pervaded this magnificent but severely furnished cham-
ber, which was only lighted by the lamp which M.
Bourigeau, the concierge, carried. A sudden dread
seized her; she shuddered, and in a faltering voice she

added: " Why are you all here? Speak, tell me what
has happened."

M. Casimir stepped forward. " A great misfortune,
mademoiselle, a terrible misfortune. The count——"

And he paused, frightened by what he was about to
say.

But Mademoiselle Marguerite had understood him.
She clasped both hands to her heart, as if she had re-
ceived a fatal wound, and uttered the single word:
" Lost! "

The next moment she turned as pale as death, her
head drooped, her eyes closed, and she staggered as if
about to fall. Two maids sprang forward to support her, but she gently repulsed them, murmuring,
" Thanks! thanks! I am strong now."

She was, in fact, sufficiently strong to conquer her
weakness. She summoned all her resolution, and, paler
than a statue, with set teeth and dry, glittering eyes,
she approached the alcove. She stood there for a moment perfectly motionless, murmuring a few unintelligi-
ble words; but at last, crushed by her sorrow, she sank
upon her knees beside the bed, buried her face in the
counterpane and wept.

Deeply moved by the sight of this despair, the servants held their breath, wondering how it would all
end. It ended suddenly. The girl sprang from her
knees, as if a gleam of hope had darted through her
heart. " A physician! " she said, eagerly.

" I have sent for one, mademoiselle," replied M.
Casimir. And hearing a voice and a sound of foot-
steps on the staircase, he added: " And fortunately,
here he comes."

The doctor entered. He was a young man, although
his head was almost quite bald. He was short, very

thin, clean-shaven, and clad in black from head to foot. Without a word, without a bow, he walked straight to the bedside, lifted the unconscious man's eyelids, felt his pulse, and uncovered his chest, applying his ear to it. "This is a serious case," he said at the close of his examination.

Mademoiselle Marguerite, who had followed his movements with the most poignant anxiety, could not repress a sob. "But all hope is not lost, is it, monsieur?" she asked in a beseeching voice, with hands clasped in passionate entreaty. "You will save him, will you not—you will save him?"

"One may always hope for the best."

This was the doctor's only answer. He had drawn his case of instruments from his pocket, and was testing the points of his lancets on the tip of his finger. When he had found one to his liking: "I must ask you, mademoiselle," said he, "to order these women to retire, and to retire yourself. The men will remain to assist me, if I require help."

She obeyed submissively, but instead of returning to her own room, she remained in the hall, seating herself upon the lower step of the staircase near the door, counting the seconds, and drawing a thousand conjectures from the slightest sound.

Meanwhile, inside the room, the physician was proceeding slowly, not from temperament however, but from principle. Dr. Jodon—for such was his name— was an ambitious man who played a part. Educated by a "prince of science," more celebrated for the money he gained than for the cures he effected, he copied his master's method, his gestures, and even the inflections of his voice. By casting in people's eyes the same powder as his teacher had employed, he hoped to obtain the same results: a large practice and an immense fortune. In his secret heart he was by no means disconcerted by his patient's condition; on the contrary, he did not consider the count's state nearly as precarious as it really was.

But bleeding and cupping alike failed to bring the sick man to consciousness. He remained speechless and motionless; the only result obtained, was that his breathing became a trifle easier. Finding his endeavors fruitless, the doctor at last declared that all immediate remedies were exhausted, that "the women" might be allowed to return, and that nothing now remained but to wait for the effect of the remedies he was about to prescribe, and which they must procure from the nearest chemist.

Any other man would have been touched by the agony of entreaty contained in the glance that Mademoiselle Marguerite cast upon the physician as she returned into the room; but it did not affect him in the least. He calmly said, "I cannot give my decision as yet."

"My God!" murmured the unhappy girl; "oh, my God, have mercy upon me!"

But the doctor, copying his model, had stationed himself near the fireplace, with his elbow leaning on the mantel-shelf, in a graceful, though rather pompous attitude. "Now," he said, addressing his remarks to M. Casimir, "I desire to make a few inquiries. Is this the first time the Count de Chalusse has had such an attack?"

"Yes, sir—at least since I have been in attendance upon him."

"Very good. That is a chance in our favor. Tell me—have you ever heard him complain of vertigo, or of a buzzing in his ears?"

" Never."

Mademoiselle Marguerite seemed inclined to volun-
teer some remark, but the doctor imposed silence upon
her by a gesture, and continued his examination. " Is
the count a great eater? " he inquired. " Does he drink
heavily? "

" The count is moderation itself, monsieur, and
he always takes a great deal of water with his
wine."

The doctor listened with an air of intent thoughtfulness, his head slightly inclined forward, his brow con-
tracted, and his under lip puffed out, while from time
to time he stroked his beardless chin. He was copying
his master. " The devil! " he said, *sotto voce*. " There
must be some cause for such an attack, however.
Nothing in the count's constitution predisposes him to
such an accident——" Then, suddenly turning toward
Mademoiselle Marguerite: " Do you know, mademoiselle, whether the count has experienced any very violent emotion during the past few days? "

" Something occurred this very morning, which
seemed to annoy him very much."

" Ah! now we have it," said the doctor, with the air
of an oracle. " Why did you not tell me all this at
first? It will be necessary for you to give me the particulars, mademoiselle."

The young girl hesitated. The servants were dazed
by the doctor's manner; but Mademoiselle Marguerite
was far from sharing their awe and admiration. She
would have given anything to have had the regular
physician of the household there instead of him! As
for this coarse examination in the presence of all these
servants, and by the bedside of a man who, in spite of
his apparent unconsciousness, was, perhaps, able to hear

and to comprehend, she looked upon it as a breach of delicacy, even of propriety.

"It is of the most urgent importance that I should be fully informed of these particulars," repeated the physician peremptorily.

After such an assertion, further hesitation was out of the question. Mademoiselle Marguerite seemed to collect her thoughts, and then she sadly said: "Just as we sat down to breakfast this morning, a letter was handed to the count. No sooner had his eyes fallen upon it, than he turned as white as his napkin. He rose from his seat and began to walk hastily up and down the dining-room, uttering exclamations of anger and sorrow. I spoke to him, but he did not seem to hear me. However, after a few moments, he resumed his seat at the table, and began to eat——"

"As usual?"

"He ate more than usual, monsieur. Only I must tell you that it seemed to me he was scarcely conscious of what he was doing. Four or five times he left the table, and then came back again. At last, after quite a struggle, he seemed to come to some decision. He tore the letter to pieces, and threw the pieces out of the window that opens upon the garden."

Mademoiselle Marguerite expressed herself with the utmost simplicity, and there was certainly nothing particularly extraordinary in her story. Still, those around her listened with breathless curiosity, as though they were expecting some startling revelation, so much does the human mind abhor that which is natural and incline to that which is mysterious.

Without seeming to notice the effect she had produced, and addressing herself to the physician alone, the girl continued: "After the letter was destroyed,

M. de Chalusse seemed himself again. Coffee was
served, and he afterward lighted a cigar as usual. However, he soon let it go out. I dared not disturb him by
any remarks; but suddenly he said to me: 'It's strange,
but I feel very uncomfortable.' A moment passed,
without either of us speaking, and then he added: 'I
am certainly not well. Will you do me the favor to
go to my room for me? Here is the key of my escritoire; open it, and on the upper shelf you will find a
small bottle which please bring to me.' I noticed with
some surprise that M. de Chalusse, who usually speaks
very distinctly, stammered and hesitated considerably in
making this request, but, unfortunately, I did not think
much about it at the time. I did as he requested, and
he poured eight or ten drops of the contents of the vial
into a glass of water, and swallowed it."

So intense was Dr. Jodon's interest that he became
himself again. He forgot to attitudinize. "And after
that?" he asked, eagerly.

"After that, M. de Chalusse seemed to feel much
better, and retired to his study as usual. I fancied that
any annoyance the letter had caused him was forgotten;
but I was wrong, for in the afternoon he sent a mes-
sage, through Madame Léon, requesting me to join him
in the garden. I hastened there, very much surprised,
for the weather was extremely disagreeable. 'Dear
Marguerite,' he said, on seeing me, 'help me to find
the fragments of that letter which I flung from the
window this morning. I would give half my fortune
for an address which it must certainly have contained,
but which I quite overlooked in my anger.' I helped
him as he asked. He might have reasonably hoped to
succeed, for it was raining when the scraps of paper
were thrown out, and instead of flying through the air,

they fell directly on to the ground. We succeeded in finding a large number of the scraps, but what M. de Chalusse so particularly wanted was not to be read on any one of them. Several times he spoke of his regret, and cursed his precipitation."

M. Bourigeau, the concierge, and M. Casimir exchanged a significant smile. They had seen the count searching for the remnants of this letter, and had thought him little better than an idiot. But now everything was explained.

" I was much grieved at the count's disappointment," continued Mademoiselle Marguerite, " but suddenly he exclaimed, joyfully: ' That address—why, such a person will give it to me—what a fool I am! ' "

The physician evinced such absorbing interest in this narrative that he forgot to retain his usual impassive attitude. " Such a person! Who— who was this person?" he inquired eagerly, without apparently realizing the impropriety of his question.

But the girl felt indignant. She silenced her indiscreet questioner with a haughty glance, and in the driest possible tone, replied: " I have forgotten the name."

Cut to the quick, the doctor suddenly resumed his master's pose; but all the same his imperturbable *sang-froid* was sensibly impaired. " Believe me, mademoiselle, that interest alone—a most respectful interest—"

She did not even seem to hear his excuse, but resumed: " I know, however, monsieur, that M. de Chalusse intended applying to the police if he failed to obtain this address from the person in question. After this he appeared to be entirely at ease. At three o'clock he rang for his valet, and ordered dinner two hours earlier than usual. We sat down to table at about half-past four. At five he rose, kissed me gayly, and left

the house on foot, telling me that he was confident of
success, and that he did not expect to return before
midnight." The poor child's firmness now gave way;
her eyes filled with tears, and it was in a voice choked
with sobs that she added, pointing to M. de Chalusse:
" But at half-past six they brought him back as you see
him now——"

An interval of silence ensued, so deep that one could
hear the faint breathing of the unconscious man still
lying motionless on his bed. However, the particulars
of the attack were yet to be learned; and it was M.
Casimir whom the physician next addressed. " What
did the driver who brought your master home say to
you?"

" Oh! almost nothing, sir; not ten words."

" You must find this man and bring him to me."

Two servants rushed out in search of him. He could
not be far away, for his vehicle was still standing in the
courtyard. They found him in a wine-shop near by.
Some of the inquisitive spectators who had been disappointed in their curiosity by Casimir's thoughtfulness
had treated him to some liquor, and in exchange he had
told them all he knew about the affair. He had quite
recovered from his fright, and was cheerful, even gay.

" Come make haste, you are wanted," said the servants.

He emptied his glass and followed them with very
bad grace, muttering and swearing between his set
teeth. The doctor, strange to say, was considerate
enough to go out into the hall to question him; but no
information of value was gained by the man's answers.
He declared that the gentleman had hired him at
twelve o'clock, hoping by this means to extort pay for
five hours' driving, which, joined to the liberal gratuity

he could not fail to obtain, would remunerate him handsomely for his day's work. Living is dear, it should be remembered, and a fellow makes as much as he can.

When the cabby had gone off, still growling, although a couple of louis had been placed in his hand, the doctor returned to his patient. He involuntarily assumed his accustomed attitude, with crossed arms, a gloomy expression of countenance, and his forehead furrowed as if with thought and anxiety. But this time he was not acting a part. In spite, or rather by reason of, the full explanation that had been given him, he found something suspicious and mysterious in the whole affair. A thousand vague and undefinable suspicions crossed his mind. Was he in presence of a crime? Certainly, evidently not. But what was the cause then of the mystery and reticence he detected? Was he upon the track of some lamentable family secret —one of those terrible scandals, concealed for a long time, but which at last burst forth with startling effect? The prospect of being mixed up in such an affair caused him infinite pleasure. It would bring him into notice; he would be mentioned in the papers; and his increased practice would fill his hands with gold.

But what could he do to ingratiate himself with these people, impose himself upon them if needs be? He reflected for some time, and finally what he thought an excellent plan occurred to him. He approached Mademoiselle Marguerite, who was weeping in an arm-chair, and touched her gently on the shoulder. She sprang to her feet at once. "One more question, mademoiselle," said he, imparting as much solemnity to his tone as he could. "Do you know what liquid it was that M. de Chalusse took this morning?"

"Alas! no, monsieur."

"It is very important that I should know. The ac-
curacy of my diagnosis is dependent upon it. What
has become of the vial?"

"I think M. de Chalusse replaced it in his escritoire."

The physician pointed to an article of furniture to
the left of the fireplace: "There?" he asked.

"Yes, monsieur."

He deliberated, but at last conquering his hesitation,
he said: "Could we not obtain this vial?"

Mademoiselle Marguerite blushed. "I haven't the
key," she faltered, in evident embarrassment.

M. Casimir approached: "It must be in the count's
pocket, and if mademoiselle will allow me——"

But she stepped back with outstretched arms as if to
protect the escritoire. "No," she exclaimed, "no—the
escritoire shall not be touched. I will not permit
it——"

"But, mademoiselle," insisted the doctor, "your
father——"

"The Count de Chalusse is not my father!"

Dr. Jodon was greatly disconcerted by Mademoiselle
Marguerite's vehemence. "Ah!" said he, in three different tones, "ah! ah!"

In less than a second, a thousand strange and con-
tradictory suppositions darted through his brain. Who,
then, could this girl be, if she were not Mademoiselle
de Chalusse? What right had she in that house? How
was it that she reigned as a sovereign there? Above
all, why this angry outburst for no other apparent cause
than a very natural and exceedingly insignificant request
on his part?

However, she had regained her self-possession, and
it was easy to see by her manner that she was seeking some means of escape from threatened danger. At

last she found it. "Casimir," she said, authoritatively, "search M. de Chalusse's pocket for the key of his escritoire."

Astonished by what he regarded as a new caprice, the valet obeyed. He gathered up the garments strewn over the floor, and eventually drew a key from one of the waistcoat pockets. Mademoiselle Marguerite took it from him, and then in a determined tone, exclaimed: " A hammer."

It was brought; whereupon, to the profound amazement of the physician, she knelt down beside the fireplace, laid the key upon one of the andirons, and with a heavy blow of the hammer, broke it into fragments. "Now," said she, quietly, "my mind will be at rest. I am certain," she added, turning toward the servants, " that M. de Chalusse would approve what I have done. When he recovers, he will have another key made."

The explanation was superfluous. All the servants understood the motive that had influenced her, and were saying to themselves, " Mademoiselle is right. It would not do to touch the escritoire of a dying man. Who knows but what there are millions in it? If anything were missed, why any of us might be accused. But if the key is destroyed, it will be impossible to suspect any one."

However, the physician's conjectures were of an entirely different nature. " What can there be in that escritoire which she desires to conceal?" he thought.

But there was no excuse for prolonging his visit. Once more he examined the sick man, whose condition remained unchanged; and then, after explaining what was to be done in his absence, he declared that he must leave at once, as he had a number of important visits to make; he added, however, that he would return about midnight.

"Madame Léon and I will watch over M. de Chalusse," replied Mademoiselle Marguerite; "that is sufficient assurance, monsieur, that your orders will be obeyed to the letter. Only—you will not take offence, I trust, if I ask the count's regular physician to meet you in consultation."

Such a proposal was anything but pleasing to M. Jodon, who had met with the same misfortune in this aristocratic neighborhood several times before. When an accident happened, he was summoned because he chanced to be close at hand, but just as he was flattering himself that he had gained a desirable patient, he found himself in presence of some celebrated physician, who had come from a distance in his carriage. Accustomed to such disappointments, he knew how to conceal his dissatisfaction.

"Were I in your place, mademoiselle, I should do precisely what you suggest," he answered, "and should you think it unnecessary for me to call, I——"

"Oh! monsieur, on the contrary, I shall certainly expect you."

"In that case, very well." Thereupon he bowed and left the room.

But Mademoiselle Marguerite followed him on to the landing. "You know, monsieur," she said, speaking rapidly in an undertone, "that I am not M. de Chalusse's daughter. You may, therefore, tell me the truth. Is his condition hopeless?"

"Alarming—yes; hopeless—no."

"But, monsieur, this terrible unconsciousness——"

"It usually follows such an attack as he has been the victim of. Still we may hope that the paralysis will

gradually disappear, and the power of motion return
after a time."

Mademoiselle Marguerite was listening, pale, agitated, and embarrassed. It was evident that she had a
question on her lips which she scarcely dared to ask.
At last, however, summoning all her courage, she exclaimed: "And if M. de Chalusse should not recover,
will he die without regaining consciousness—without
being able to speak?"

"I am unable to say, mademoiselle—the count's mal-
ady is one of those which set at naught all the hypoth-
eses of science."

She thanked him sadly, sent a servant to summon
Madame Léon, and returned to the count's room.

As for the doctor, he said to himself as he went
downstairs, "What a strange girl! Is she afraid that
the count will regain consciousness? or, on the contrary, does she wish him to speak? Is there any question of a will under all this? What else can it be?
What is at stake?" His preoccupation was so intense
that he almost forgot where he was going, and he
paused on every step. It was not until the fresh air
of the courtyard blew upon his face, reminding him of
the realities of life, that the charlatanesque element in
his nature regained the ascendency. "My friend," he
said, addressing M. Casimir, who was lighting him out,
"you must at once have some straw spread over the
street so as to deaden the sound of the vehicles. And
to-morrow, you must inform the commissary of police."

Ten minutes later a thick bed of straw had been
strewed across the thoroughfare, and the drivers of
passing vehicles involuntarily slackened their speed, for
every one in Paris knows what this signifies. M. Casimir personally superintended the work which was in-

trusted to the grooms, and he was about to return
indoors again, when a young man, who had been walking up and down in front of the mansion for more
than an hour, hastily approached him. He was a beardless fellow with a strangely wrinkled face, as leaden-
tinted as that of a confirmed absinthe-drinker. His general expression was shrewd, and at the same time im-
pudent, and surprising audacity gleamed in his eyes.
" What do you want? " asked M. Casimir.

The young fellow bowed humbly, and replied, " Ah,
don't you recognize me, monsieur? I'm Toto—excuse
me—Victor Chupin, employed by M. Isidore Fortunat."

" Oh, yes. I recollect."

" I came, in obedience to my employer's orders, to
inquire if you had obtained the information you promised him; but seeing that something had happened at
your house, I didn't dare go in, but decided to watch
for you——"

" And you did quite right, my lad. I have no information to give you—ah, yes! stop! The Marquis
de Valorsay was closeted with the count for two hours
yesterday. But what good will that do? The count has
been taken suddenly ill, and he will scarcely live through
the night."

Victor Chupin was thunderstruck. " Impossible! "
he cried. " Is it for him that the straw has been
strewed in the street? "

" It's for him."

" What a lucky fellow! No one would go to such
expense for me! But I have an idea that my guv'nor
will hardly laugh when I tell him this. Still, thank you
all the same, m'sieur, and *au revoir*." He was darting
off when a sudden thought detained him. " Excuse
me," said he, with conjuror like volubility; " I was so

horrified that I forgot business. Tell me, m'sieur, if
the count dies, you'll take charge of the funeral arrangements, won't you? Very well; a word of advice
then. Don't go to the regular undertakers, but come
to me: here's my address"—proffering a card—"I
will treat with the undertakers for you, and take charge
of everything. It will be much better and far cheaper
for you, on account of certain arrangements I've made
with these parties. Everything, to the very last plume,
is warranted to give perfect satisfaction. Each item
will be specified in the bill, and can be verified during
the ceremony, no payment exacted until after delivery.
Well, is it understood?"

The valet shrugged his shoulders. "Nonsense!"
said he, carelessly; "what is all that to me?"

"Ah! I forgot to mention that there would be a
commission of two hundred francs to divide between
us."

"That's consideration. Give me your card, and rely
on me. My compliments to M. Fortunat, please." And
so saying, he re-entered the house.

Victor Chupin drew a huge silver watch from his
pocket and consulted it. "Five minutes to eight," he
growled, "and the guv'nor expects me at eight precisely. I shall have to stretch out my legs."

II.

M. ISIDORE FORTUNAT resided at No. 27 Place de la Bourse, on the third floor. He had a handsome suite of apartments : a drawing-room, a dining-room, a bedroom, a large outer office where his clerks worked, and a private one, which was the sanctuary of his thoughts and meditations. The whole cost him only six thousand francs a year, a mere trifle as rents go nowadays. His lease entitled him, moreover, to the use of a room ten feet square, up under the eaves, where he lodged his servant, Madame Dodelin, a woman of forty-six or thereabouts, who had met with reverses of fortune, and who now took such good charge of his establishment, that his table—for he ate at home—was truly fit for a sybarite.

Having been established here for five years or more, M. Fortunat was very well known in the neighborhood, and, as he paid his rent promptly, and met all his obligations without demur, he was generally respected. Besides, people knew very well from what source M. Fortunat derived his income. He gave his attention to contested claims, liquidations, the recovery of legacies, and so on, as was shown by the inscription in large letters which figured on the elegant brass plate adorning his door. He must have had a prosperous business, for he employed six collectors in addition to the clerks who wrote all day long in his office; and his clients were so numerous that the concierge was often heard to complain of the way they ran up and down the stairs, declaring that it was worse than a procession.

To be just, we must add that M. Fortunat's appear-

ance, manners and conduct were of a nature to quiet
all suspicions.   He was some thirty-eight years of age,
extremely methodical in his habits, gentle and refined
in his manner, intelligent, very good-looking, and always dressed in perfect taste.   He was accused of
being, in business matters, as cold, as polished, and as
hard as one of the marble slabs of the Morgue; but
then, no one was obliged to employ him unless they
chose to do so.   This much is certain: he did not frequent *cafés* or places of amusement.   If he went out
at all after dinner, it was only to pass the evening at
the house of some rich client in the neighborhood.   He
detested the smell of tobacco, and was inclined to
be devout—never failing to attend eight o'clock mass
on Sunday mornings.   His housekeeper suspected
him of matrimonial designs, and perhaps she was
right.

On the evening that the Count de Chalusse was
struck with apoplexy M. Isidore Fortunat had been
dining alone and was sipping a cup of tea when the
door-bell rang, announcing the arrival of a visitor.
Madame Dodelin hastened to open the door, and in
walked Victor Chupin, breathless from his hurried walk.
It had not taken him twenty-five minutes to cover the
distance which separates the Rue de Courcelles from
the Place de la Bourse.

" You are late, Victor," said M. Fortunat, quietly.

" That's true, monsieur, but it isn't my fault.   Everything was in confusion down there, and I was obliged
to wait——"

" How is that?   Why?"

" The Count de Chalusse was stricken with apoplexy
this evening, and he is probably dead by this time."

M. Fortunat sprang from his chair with a livid face

and trembling lips. "Stricken with apoplexy!" he exclaimed in a husky voice. "I am ruined!"

Then, fearing Madame Dodelin's curiosity, he seized the lamp and rushed into his office, crying to Chupin: "Follow me."

Chupin obeyed without a word, for he was a shrewd fellow, and knew how to make the best of a trying situation. He was not usually allowed to enter this private room, the floor of which was covered with a magnificent carpet; and so, after carefully closing the door, he remained standing, hat in hand, and looking somewhat intimidated. But M. Fortunat seemed to have forgotten his presence. After depositing the lamp on the mantel-shelf, he walked several times round and round the room like a hunted beast seeking for some means of egress.

"If the count is dead," he muttered, "the Marquis de Valorsay is lost! Farewell to the millions!"

The blow was so cruel, and so entirely unexpected, that he could not, would not believe in its reality. He walked straight to Chupin, and caught him by the collar, as if the young fellow had been the cause of this misfortune. "It isn't possible," said he; "the count *cannot* be dead. You are deceiving me, or they deceived you. You must have misunderstood—you only wished to give some excuse for your delay perhaps. Speak, say something!"

As a rule, Chupin was not easily impressed, but he felt almost frightened by his employer's agitation. "I only repeated what M. Casimir told me, monsieur," was his reply.

He then wished to furnish some particulars, but M. Fortunat had already resumed his furious tramp to and fro, giving vent to his wrath and despair in incoherent

exclamations. "Forty thousand francs lost!" he exclaimed. "Forty thousand francs, counted out there
on my desk! I see them yet, counted and placed in the
hand of the Marquis de Valorsay in exchange for his
signature. My savings for a number of years, and I
have only a worthless scrap of paper to show for them.
That cursed marquis! And he was to come here this
evening, and I was to give him ten thousand francs
more. They are lying there in that drawer. Let him
come, the wretch, let him come!"

Anger had positively brought foam to M. Fortunat's
lips, and any one seeing him then would subsequently
have had but little confidence in his customary good-
natured air and unctuous politeness. "And yet the
marquis is as much to be pitied as I am," he continued.
"He loses as much, even more! And such a sure thing
it seemed, too! What speculation can a fellow engage
in after this? And a man must put his money some
where; he can't bury it in the ground!"

Chupin listened with an air of profound commiseration; but it was only assumed. He was inwardly jubi-
lant, for his interest in the affair was in direct opposi-
tion to that of his employer. Indeed, if M. Fortunat
lost forty thousand francs by the Count de Chalusse's
death, Chupin expected to make a hundred francs commission on the funeral.

"Still, he may have made a will!" pursued M.
Fortunat. "But no, I'm sure he hasn't. A poor devil
who has only a few sous to leave behind him always
takes this precaution. He thinks he may be run over
by an omnibus and suddenly killed, and he always
writes and signs his last wishes. But millionaires don't
think of such things; they believe themselves im-
mortal!" He paused to reflect for a moment, for

power of reflection had returned to him. His excitement had quickly spent itself by reason of its very violence. " This much is certain," he resumed, slowly, and in a more composed voice, " whether the count has made a will or not, Valorsay will lose the millions he expected from Chalusse. If there is no will, Mademoiselle Marguerite won't have a sou, and then, good evening! If there is one, this devil of a girl, suddenly becoming her own mistress, and wealthy into the bargain, will send Monsieur de Valorsay about his business, especially if she loves another, as he himself admits— and in that case, again good evening! "

M. Fortunat drew out his handkerchief, and, pausing in front of the looking-glass, wiped the perspiration from his brow, and arranged his disordered hair. He was one of those men who may be stunned, but never crushed, by a catastrophe. " In conclusion," he muttered, " I must enter my forty thousand francs as an item in the profit and loss account. It only remains to be seen if it would not be possible to regain them in the same affair." He was again master of himself, and never had his mind been more clear. He seated himself at his desk, leant his elbows upon it, rested his head on his hands, and remained for some time perfectly motionless; but there was triumph in his gesture when he at last looked up again.

" I am safe," he muttered, so low that Chupin could not hear him. " What a fool I was! If there is no will a fourth of the millions shall be mine! Ah, when a man knows his ground, he never need lose the battle! But I must act quickly," he added, "very quickly." And so speaking, he rose and glanced at the clock. " Nine o'clock," said he. " I must open the campaign this very evening."

Motionless in his dark corner, Chupin still retained his commiserating attitude; but he was so oppressed with curiosity that he could scarcely breathe. He opened his eyes and ears to the utmost, and watched his employer's slightest movements with intense interest.

Prompt to act when he had once decided upon his course, M. Fortunat now drew from his desk a large portfolio, crammed full of letters, receipts, bills, deeds of property, and old parchments. " I can certainly discover the necessary pretext here," he murmured, rummaging through the mass of papers. But he did not at once find what he sought, and he was growing impatient, as could be seen by his feverish haste, when all at once he paused with a sigh of relief. " At last! "

He held in his hand a soiled and crumpled note of hand, affixed by a pin to a huissier's protest, thus proving conclusively that it had been dishonored. M. Fortunat waved these strips of paper triumphantly, and with a satisfied air exclaimed: " It is here that I must strike; it is here—if Casimir hasn't deceived me —that I shall find the indispensable information I need."

He was in such haste that he did not wait to put his portfolio in order. He threw it with the papers it had contained into the drawer of his desk again, and, approaching Chupin, he asked, " It was you, was it not, Victor, who obtained that information respecting the solvency of the Vantrassons, husband and wife, who let out furnished rooms? "

" Yes, monsieur, and I gave you the answer: nothing to hope for——"

" I know; but that doesn't matter. Do you remember their address? "

" Perfectly. They are now living on the Asnières

Road, beyond the fortifications, on the right hand side."

" What is the number ? "

Chupin hesitated, reflected for a moment, and then began to scratch his head furiously, as he was in the habit of doing whenever his memory failed him and he wished to recall it to duty. " I'm not sure whether the number is eighteen or forty-six," he said, at last; " that is——"

" Never mind," interrupted M. Fortunat. " If I sent you to the house could you find it ? "

" Oh—yes, m'sieur—at once—with my eyes shut. I can see the place perfectly—a rickety old barrack. There is a tract of unoccupied land on one s\de, and a kitchen-garden in the rear."

" Very well; you shall accompany me there."

Chupin seemed astonished by this strange proposal. " What, m'sieur," said he, " do you think of going there at this time of night ? "

" Why not ? Shall we find the establishment closed ?"

" No; certainly not. Vantrasson doesn't merely keep furnished rooms; he's a grocer, and sells liquor too. His place is open until eleven o'clock at least. But if you are going there to present a bill, it's perhaps a little late. If I were in your place, m'sieur, I should wait till to-morrow. It's raining, and the streets are deserted. It's an out-of-the-way place too; and in such cases, a man has been known to settle his account with whatever came handiest—with a cudgel, or a bullet, for instance."

" Are you afraid ? "

This question seemed so utterly absurd to Chupin that he was not in the least offended by it; his only answer was a disdainful shrug of the shoulders.

" Then we will go," remarked M. Fortunat. " While

I'm getting ready, go and hire a cab, and see that you get a good horse."

Chupin was off in an instant, tearing down the staircase like a tempest. There was a cab-stand only a few steps from the house, but he preferred to run to the jobmaster's stables in the Rue Feydeau.

" Cab, sir ! " shouted several men, as they saw him approaching.

He made no reply, but began to examine the horses with the air of a connoisseur, until at last he found an animal that suited him. Thereupon he beckoned to the driver, and going to the little office where a woman sat reading: " My five sous, if you please," he said, authoritatively.

The woman looked at him. Most jobmasters are in the habit of giving five sous to any servant who comes in search of a cab for his master; and this was the custom here. But the keeper of the office, who felt sure that Chupin was not a servant, hesitated; and this made the young fellow angry. " Make haste," he cried, imperiously. " If you don't, I shall run to the nearest stand."

The woman at once threw him five sous, which he pocketed with a satisfied grin. They were his—rightfully his—since he had taken the trouble to gain them. He then hastily returned to the office to inform his employer that the cab was waiting at the door, and found himself face to face with a sight which made him open his eyes to their widest extent.

M. Fortunat had profited by his clerk's absence, not to disguise himself—that would be saying too much— but to make some changes in his appearance. He had arrayed himself in a long overcoat, shiny with grease and wear, and falling below his knees; in place of his

elegant satin cravat he had knotted a gaudy silk necker-
chief about his throat; his boots were worn, and out
of shape; and his hat would have been treated with
contempt even by a dealer in old clothes. Of the prosperous Fortunat, so favorably known round about the
·Place de la Bourse, naught remained save his face and
his hands. Another Fortunat had taken his place, more
than needy in aspect—wretched, famished, gaunt with
hunger, ready for any desperate deed. And, yet, he
seemed at ease in this garb; it yielded to his every
movement, as if he had worn it for a long time. The
butterfly had become a chrysalis again. Chupin's ad-
miring smile must have repaid him for his trouble.
Since the young clerk evinced approval, M. Fortunat
felt sure that Vantrasson would take him for what he
wished to appear—a poor devil of an agent, who was
acting on some other person's behalf. "Let us start
at once," said he.

But just as he was leaving the ante-room, he remembered an order of great importance which he wished to
give. He called Madame Dodelin, and without paying
the slightest heed to her astonishment at seeing him
thus attired: "If the Marquis de Valorsay comes, in
my absence," said he—"and he *will* come—ask him to
wait for me. I shall return before midnight. Don't take
him into my office—he can wait in the drawing-room."

This last order was certainly unnecessary, since M.
Fortunat had closed and double-locked his office door,
and placed the key carefully in his own pocket. But
perhaps he had forgotten this circumstance. There
were now no traces of his recent anger and disappointment. He was in excellent humor; and you might
have supposed that he was starting on an enterprise from
which he expected to derive both pleasure and profit.

Chupin was climbing to a place on the box beside the driver when his employer bade him take a seat inside the vehicle. They were not long in reaching their destination, for the horse was really a good one, and the driver had been stimulated by the promise of a magnificent gratuity. In fact, M. Fortunat and his companion reached the Asnières Road in less than forty minutes.

In obedience to the orders he had received before starting, the cabman drew up on the right hand side of the road, at about a hundred paces from the city gate, beyond the fortifications. " Well, sir, here you are! Are you satisfied?" he inquired, as he opened the door.

" Perfectly satisfied," replied M. Fortunat. " Here is your promised gratuity. Now, you have only to wait for us. Don't stir from this place. Do you understand?"

But the driver shook his head. " Excuse me," he said, " but if it's all the same to you, I will station myself over there near the gate. Here, you see, I should be afraid to go to sleep, while over there——"

" Very well; suit yourself," M. Fortunat replied.

This precaution on the driver's part convinced him that Chupin had not exaggerated the evil reputation of this quarter of the Parisian suburbs. And, indeed, there was little of a reassuring character in the aspect of this broad road, quite deserted at this hour, and shrouded in the darkness of a tempestuous night. The rain had ceased falling, but the wind blew with increased violence, twisting the branches off the trees, tearing slates from the roofs, and shaking the street-lamps so furiously as to extinguish the gas. They could not see a step before them; the mud was ankle-deep, and not a person, not a solitary soul was visible.

"Are we almost there?" M. Fortunat asked every ten paces.

"Almost there, m'sieur."

Chupin said this; but to tell the truth, he knew nothing about it. He tried to discover where he was, but did not succeed. Houses were becoming scanty, and vacant plots of building ground more numerous; it was only with the greatest difficulty that one could occasionally discern a light. At last, however, after a quarter of an hour's hard struggling, Chupin uttered a joyful cry. "Here we are, m'sieur—look!" said he.

A large building, five stories high, sinister of aspect, and standing quite alone, could just be distinguished in the darkness. It was already falling to pieces, and yet it was not entirely completed. Plainly enough, the speculator who had undertaken the enterprise had not been rich enough to complete it. On seeing the many closely pierced windows of the façade, a passer-by could not fail to divine for what purpose the building had been erected; and in order that no one should remain in ignorance of it, this inscription : "Furnished Rooms," figured in letters three feet high, between the third and fourth floors. The inside arrangements could be easily divined : innumerable rooms, all small and inconvenient, and let out at exorbitant rentals.

However, Victor Chupin's memory had misled him. This establishment was not on the right, but on the left-hand side of the road, a perfect mire through which M. Fortunat and his companion were obliged to cross. Their eyes having become accustomed to the darkness, they could discern sundry details as they approached the building. The ground floor comprised two shops, one of which was closed, but the other was still open, and a faint light gleamed through the soiled red curtains. Over the frontage appeared the shop-keeper's name, Vantrasson, while on either side, in smaller letters, were the words: "Groceries and Pro-visions—Foreign and French Wines." Everything about this den denoted abject poverty and low de-bauchery.

M. Fortunat certainly did not recoil, but before en-tering the shop he was not sorry to have an opportunity to reconnoitre. He approached cautiously, and peered through the window at a place where a rent in the cur-tain allowed him some view of the interior. Behind the counter a woman who looked some fifty years of age was seated, mending a soiled dress by the light of a smoking lamp. She was short and very stout. She seemed literally weighed down, and puffed out by an unwholesome and unnatural mass of superfluous flesh; and she was as white as if her veins had been filled with water, instead of blood. Her hanging cheeks, her receding forehead, and her thin lips, imparted an alarm-ing expression of wickedness and cunning to her countenance. At the farther end of the store For-tunat could vaguely discern the figure of a man seated on a stool. He seemed to be asleep, for his crossed arms rested on a table, with his head leaning on them.

"Good luck!" whispered Chupin in his employer's ear; "there is not a customer in the place. Vantrasson and his wife are alone." This circumstance was by no means displeasing to M. Fortunat, as could be seen by his expression of face. "So, m'sieur," continued Chu-pin, "you need have no fears. I'll remain here and watch, while you go in."

M. Fortunat did so. On hearing the door open and

shut, the woman laid down her work. "What can I
do for monsieur?" she asked, in a wheedling voice.

M. Fortunat did not reply at once; but he drew the
note with which he had provided himself from his
pocket, and displayed it. "I am a huissier's clerk,"
he then exclaimed; "and I called in reference to this
little matter—a note of hand for five hundred and
eighty-three francs, value received in goods, signed
Vantrasson, and made payable to the order of a person
named Barutin."

"An execution!" said the woman, whose voice suddenly soured. "Vantrasson, wake up, and come and
see about this."

This summons was unnecessary. On hearing the
words "note of hand," the man had lifted his head;
and at the name of Barutin, he rose and approached
with a heavy, uncertain step, as if he had not yet slept
off his intoxication. He was younger than his wife,
tall, with a well-proportioned and athletic form. His
features were regular, but the abuse of alcohol and
all sorts of excesses had greatly marred them, and their
present expression was one of ferocious brutishness.
"What's that you are talking about?" he asked in a
harsh, grating voice. "Is it to mock people that you
come and ask for money on the 15th of October—rent
day? Where have you seen any money left after the
landlord has made his round? Besides, what is this
bill? Give it me to look at."

M. Fortunat was not guilty of such folly; he did not
intrust the paper to Vantrasson's hand, but held it a
little distance from him, and then read it aloud.

When he had finished: "That note fell due eighteen
months ago," declared Vantrasson. "It is worth
nothing now——"

"WHAT IS THIS BILL? GIVE IT ME TO LOOK AT"

" You are mistaken—a note of this kind is of value any time within five years after the day it goes to protest."

" Possibly; but as Barutin has failed, and gone no one knows where, I am released——"

" Another mistake on your part. You owe these five hundred and eighty-three francs to the person who bought this note at Barutin's sale, and who has given my employer orders to prosecute——"

The blood had risen to Vantrasson's face. "And what of that? Do you suppose I've never been sued for debts before? Even the king can't take anything from a person who possesses nothing; and I own nothing. My furniture is all pawned or mortgaged, and my stock is not worth a hundred francs. When your employer finds it useless to waste money in worrying me, he'll let me alone. You can't injure a man like me."

" Do you really think so?"

" I'm sure of it."

" Unfortunately you are again mistaken, for although the holder of the note doesn't care so very much about obtaining his dues, he'll spend his own money like water to make trouble for you." And thereupon M. Fortunat began to draw a vivid and frightful picture of a poor debtor pursued by a rich creditor who harassed him, and tortured him, and hounded him everywhere, until not even a change of clothing was left him.

Vantrasson rolled his eyes and brandished his formidable fist in the most defiant manner; but his wife was evidently much alarmed. At last she could bear it no longer, and rising hastily she led her husband to the rear of the shop, saying: " Come, I must speak with you."

He followed her, and they remained for some little time conversing together in a low tone, but with excited gestures. When they returned, the woman opened the conversation. "Alas! sir," she said to M. Fortunat, "we have no money just now; business is so very bad, and if you prosecute us, we are lost. What can be done? You look like an honest man; give us your advice."

M. Fortunat did not reply at once; he was apparently absorbed in thought, but suddenly he exclaimed: "One owes a duty to unfortunate folks, and I'm going to tell you the exact truth. My employer, who isn't a bad man at heart, hasn't the slightest desire for revenge. He said to me: ' Go and see these Vantrassons, and if they seem to be worthy people, propose a compromise. If they choose to accept it, I shall be quite satisfied.' "

"And what is this compromise?"

"It is this: you must write an acknowledgment of the debt on a sheet of stamped paper, together with a promise to pay a little on account each month. In exchange I will give you this note of hand."

The husband and wife exchanged glances, and it was the woman who said: "We accept."

But to carry out this arrangement it was necessary to have a sheet of stamped paper, and the spurious clerk had neglected to provide himself with some. This circumstance seemed to annoy him greatly, and you might almost have sworn that he regretted the concession he had promised. Did he think of going? Madame Vantrasson feared so, and turning eagerly to her husband, she exclaimed: "Run to the tobacco shop in the Rue de Levis; you will find some paper there!"

He started off at once, and M. Fortunat breathed freely again. He had certainly retained his composure admirably during the interview, but more than once he had fancied that Vantrasson was about to spring on him, crush him with his brawny hands, tear the note from him, burn it, and then throw him, Fortunat, out into the street, helpless and nearly dead. But now that danger had passed and Madame Vantrasson, fearing he might tire of waiting, was prodigal in her attentions. She brought him the only unbroken chair in the establishment, and insisted that he should partake of some refreshment—a glass of wine at the very least. While rummaging among the bottles, she alternately thanked him and complained, declaring she had a right to repine, since she had known better days—but fate had been against her ever since her marriage, though she had little thought she would end her days in such misery, after having been so happy in the Count de Chalusse's household many years before.

To all appearance, M. Fortunat listened with the mere superficial interest which ordinary politeness requires one to show, but in reality his heart was filled with intense delight. Coming here without any clearly-defined plan, circumstances had served him a thousand times better than he could reasonably have hoped. He had preserved his power over the Vantrassons, had won their confidence, had succeeded in obtaining a *tête-à-tête* with the wife, and to crown all, this woman alluded, of her own accord, to the very subject upon which he was longing to question her.

"Ah! if I were only back in the Count's household again," she exclaimed. "Six hundred francs a year, and gifts worth double that amount. Those were good times for me. But you know how it is—one is never content with one's lot, and then the heart is weak——"

She had not succeeded in finding the sweet wine

which she proposed to her guest; so in its place she substituted a mixture of ratafia and brandy in two large glasses which she placed upon the counter. " One evening, to my sorrow," she resumed, " I met Vantrasson at a ball. It was the 13th day of the month. I might have known no good would come of it. Ah, you should have seen him at that time, in full uniform. He belonged to the Paris Guards then. All the women were crazy about soldiers, and my head was turned, too——" Her tone, her gestures, and the compression of her thin lips, revealed the bitterness of her disappointment and her unavailing regret. " Ah, these handsome men!" she continued; " don't talk to me about them! This one had heard of my savings. I had nineteen thousand francs, so he begged me to marry him, and I was fool enough to consent. Yes, fool—for I was forty, and he was only thirty. I might have known it was my money that he wanted, and not me. However, I gave up my situation, and even purchased a substitute for him, in order that I might have him all to myself."

She had gradually warmed with her theme, as she described her confidence and blind credulity, and then, with a tragic gesture, as if she desired to drive away these cruel memories, she suddenly seized her glass and emptied it at a draught.

Chupin, who was still at his post outside, experienced a thrill of envy, and involuntarily licked his lips. " A mixed ratafia," he said, longingly. " I shouldn't object to one myself."

However, this choice compound seemed to inspire Madame Vantrasson with renewed energy, for, with still greater earnestness, she resumed: " At first, all went well. We employed my savings in purchasing the

Hôtel des Espagnes, in the Rue Notre Dame des Victoires, and business prospered; there was never a vacant room. But any person who has drank, sir, will drink again. Vantrasson kept sober for a few months, but gradually he fell into his old habits. He was in such a condition most of the time that he was scarcely able to ask for food. And if that had been all! But, unfortunately, he was too handsome a man to be a good husband. One night he didn't come home, and the next day, when I ventured to reproach him—very gently, I assure you—he answered me with an oath and a blow. All our happiness was over! Monsieur declared that he was master, and would do as he liked. He drank and carried away all the wine from the cellar— he took all the money—he remained away for weeks together; and if I complained—more blows!"

Her voice trembled, and a tear gathered in her eye; but, wiping it away with the back of her hand, she resumed: "Vantrasson was always drunk, and I spent my time in crying my very eyes out. Business became very bad, and soon everybody left the house. We were obliged to sell it. We did so, and bought a small *café*. But by the end of the year we lost that. Fortunately, I still had a little money left, and so I bought a stock of groceries in my own name; but in less than six months the stock was eaten up, and we were cast into the street. What was to be done? Vantrasson drank worse than ever; he demanded money when he knew that I had none to give him, and he treated me even more cruelly than before. I lost courage—and yet one must live! Oh, you wouldn't believe it if I told you how we have lived for the past four years." She did not tell him, but contented herself with adding, "When you begin to go down hill, there is no such thing as stopping; you roll lower and lower, until you reach the bottom, as we have done. Here we live, no one knows how; we have to pay our rent each week, and if we are driven from this place, I see no refuge but the river."

"If I had been in your position, I should have left my husband," M. Fortunat ventured to remark.

"Yes—it would have been better, no doubt. People advised me to do so, and I tried. Three or four times I went away, and yet I always returned—it was stronger than myself. Besides, I'm his wife; I've paid dearly for him; he's mine—I won't yield him to any one else. He beats me, no doubt; I despise him, I hate him, and yet I——" She poured out part of a glass of brandy, and swallowed it; then, with a gesture of rage, she added: "I can't give him up! It's fate! As it is now, it will be until the end, until he starves, or I——"

M. Fortunat's countenance wore an expression of profound commiseration. A looker-on would have supposed him interested and sympathetic to the last degree; but in reality, he was furious. Time was passing, and the conversation was wandering farther and farther from the object of his visit. "I am surprised, madame," said he, "that you never applied to your former employer, the Count de Chalusse."

"Alas! I did apply to him for assistance several times——"

"With what result?"

"The first time I went to him he received me; I told him my troubles, and he gave me bank-notes to the amount of five thousand francs."

M. Fortunat raised his hands to the ceiling. "Five thousand francs!" he repeated, in a tone of astonishment; "this count must be very rich——"

"So rich, monsieur, that he doesn't know how much he's worth. He owns, nobody knows how many houses in Paris, châteaux in every part of the country, entire villages, forests—his gold comes in by the shovelful."

The spurious clerk closed his eyes, as if he were dazzled by this vision of wealth.

"The second time I went to the count's house," resumed Madame Vantrasson, "I didn't see him, but he sent me a thousand francs. The third and last time they gave me twenty francs at the door, and told me that the count had gone on a journey. I understood that I could hope for no further help from him. Besides, all the servants had been changed. One morning, without any apparent reason, M. de Chalusse dismissed all the old servants, so they told me. He even sent away the concierge and the housekeeper."

"Why didn't you apply to his wife?"

"M. de Chalusse isn't married. He never has been married."

From the expression of solicitude upon her guest's features, Madame Vantrasson supposed he was racking his brain to discover some mode of escape from her present difficulties. "If I were in your place," he said, "I should try to interest his relatives and family in my case——"

"The count has no relatives."

"Impossible!"

"He hasn't, indeed. During the ten years I was in his service, I heard him say more than a dozen times that he alone was left of all his family—that all the others were dead. People pretend that this is the reason why he is so immensely rich."

M. Fortunat's interest was no longer assumed; he was rapidly approaching the real object of his visit.

"No relatives!" he muttered. "Who, then, will inherit his millions when he dies?"

Madame Vantrasson jerked her head. "Who can say?" she replied. "Everything will go to the government, probably, unless—— But no, that's impossible."

"What's impossible?"

"Nothing. I was thinking of the count's sister, Mademoiselle Hermine."

"His sister! Why, you said just now that he had no relatives."

"It's the same as if he hadn't; no one knows what has become of her, poor creature! Some say that she married; others declare that she died. It's quite a romance."

M. Isidore Fortunat was literally upon the rack; and to make his sufferings still more horrible, he dared not ask any direct question, nor allow his curiosity to become manifest, for fear of alarming the woman. "Let me see," said he; "I think—I am sure that I have heard—or that I have read—I cannot say which—some story about a Mademoiselle de Chalusse. It was something terrible, wasn't it?"

"Terrible, indeed. But what I was speaking of happened a long time ago—twenty-five or twenty-six years ago, at the very least. I was still in my own part of the country—at Besançon. No one knows the exact truth about the affair."

"What! not even you?"

"Oh! I—that's an entirely different thing. When I entered the count's service, six years later, there was still an old gardener who knew the whole story, and who told it to me, making me swear that I would never betray his confidence."

Lavish of details as she had been in telling her own story, it was evident that she was determined to exercise a prudent reserve in everything connected with the De Chalusse family; and M. Fortunat inwardly cursed this, to him, most unseasonable discretion. But he was experienced in these examinations, and he had at his command little tricks for loosening tongues, which even an investigating magistrate might have envied. Without seeming to attach the slightest importance to Madame Vantrasson's narrative, he rose with a startled air, like a man who suddenly realizes that he has forgotten himself. "Zounds!" he exclaimed, "we sit here gossiping, and it's growing late. I really can't wait for your husband. If I remain here any longer, I shall miss the last omnibus; and I live on the other side of the river, near the Luxembourg."

"But our agreement, monsieur?"

"We will draw that up at some future time. I shall be passing again, or I will send one of my colleagues to see you."

It was Madame Vantrasson's turn to tremble now. She feared, if she allowed this supposed clerk to go without signing the agreement, that the person who came in his stead might not prove so accommodating; and even if he called again himself, he might not be so kindly disposed. "Wait just a moment longer, monsieur," she pleaded; "my husband will soon be back, and the last omnibus doesn't leave the Rue de Levis until midnight."

"I wouldn't refuse, but this part of the suburbs is so lonely."

"Vantrasson will see you on your way." And, resolved to detain him at any cost, she poured out a fresh glass of liquor for him, and said: "Where were we?

Oh, yes! I was about to tell you Mademoiselle Hermine's story."

Concealing his delight with an assumed air of resignation, M. Fortunat reseated himself, to the intense disgust of Chupin, who was thoroughly tired of waiting outside in the cold.

"I must tell you," began Madame Vantrasson, "that when this happened—at least twenty-five years ago—the De Chalusse family lived in the Rue Saint-Dominique. They occupied a superb mansion, with extensive grounds, full of splendid trees like those in the Tuileries gardens. Mademoiselle Hermine, who was then about eighteen or nineteen years old, was, according to all accounts, the prettiest young creature ever seen. Her skin was as white as milk, she had a profusion of golden hair, and her eyes were as blue as forget-me-nots. She was very kind and generous, they say, only, like all the rest of the family, she was very haughty and obstinate—oh, obstinate enough to allow herself to be roasted alive over a slow fire rather than yield an inch. That's the count's nature exactly. Having served him, I know something about it, to be sure, and——"

"Excuse me," interrupted M. Fortunat, who was determined to prevent these digressions, "and Mademoiselle Hermine?"

"I was coming to her. Although she was very beautiful and immensely rich, she had no suitors—for it was generally understood that she was to marry a marquis, whose father was a particular friend of the family. The parents had arranged the matter between them years before, and nothing was wanting but the young lady's consent; but Mademoiselle Hermine absolutely refused to hear the marquis's name mentioned.

They did everything to persuade her to consent to this marriage; they employed prayers and threats alike, but they might as well have talked to a stone. When they asked her why she refused to marry the marquis, she replied, ' Because '—and that was all. In fact, at last she declared she would leave home and take refuge in a convent, if they didn't cease to torment her. Her relatives were certain there must be some reason for her refusal. It isn't natural for a girl to reject a suitor who is young, handsome, rich, and a marquis besides. Her friends suspected there was something she wouldn't confess; and M. Raymond swore that he would watch his sister, and discover her secret."

" M. Raymond is the present Count de Chalusse, I suppose?" inquired M. Fortunat.

" Yes, monsieur. Such was the state of matters when, one night, the gardener thought he heard a noise in the pavilion, at the end of the garden. This pavilion was very large. I have seen it. It contained a sitting-room, a billiard-room, and a large fencing-hall. Naturally enough, the gardener got up to go and see what was the matter. As he left the house, he fancied he saw two persons moving about among the trees. He ran after them, but could find nothing. They had made their escape through a small gate leading from the garden into the street. When the gardener was telling me this story, he declared again and again that he had fancied the noise he had heard was made by some of the servants trying to leave the house secretly, and for this reason he didn't give the alarm. However, he hurried to the pavilion, but on seeing no light there, he went back to bed with an easy mind."

" And it was Mademoiselle Hermine eloping with a lover?" asked M. Fortunat.

Madame Vantrasson seemed as disappointed as an
actor who has been deprived of an opportunity of pro-
ducing a grand effect. " Wait a moment," she replied, " and you'll see. The night passed, morning
came, and then the breakfast hour. But Mademoiselle
Hermine did not make her appearance. Some one was
sent to rap at her door—there was no answer. The
door was opened—the young lady was not in her room,
and the bed had not even been disturbed. In a few
moments the whole household was in the wildest commotion; the mother weeping, and the father half wild
with rage and sorrow. Of course, the next thought
was of Mademoiselle Hermine's brother, and he was
sent for. But, he, too, was not in his room, and his
bed had not been touched. The excitement was becoming frenzy, when it occurred to the gardener to mention what he had heard and seen on the previous night.
They hastened to the pavilion, and discovered what?
Why, M. Raymond stretched upon the ground, stiff,
cold, and motionless, weltering in his own blood. One
of his rigid hands still grasped a sword. They lifted
him up, carried him to the house, laid him upon his
bed, and sent for a physician. He had received two
dangerous wounds; one in the throat, the other in the
breast. For more than a month he hung between life
and death, and six weeks elapsed before he had strength
to relate what had happened. He was lighting a cigar
at his window when he thought he saw a woman's form
flit through the garden. A suspicion that it might be
his sister flashed through his mind; so he hastened
down, stole noiselessly into the pavilion, and there he
found his sister and a young man who was absolutely
unknown to him. He might have killed the intruder,
but instead of doing so, he told him they would fight

then and there. Weapons were within reach, and they fought, with the result that Raymond was wounded twice, in quick succession, and fell. His adversary, supposing him dead, thereupon fled from the spot, taking Mademoiselle Hermine with him."

At this point in her narrative Madame Vantrasson evinced a desire to pause and draw a breath, and perhaps partake of some slight refreshment; but M. Fortunat was impatient. The woman's husband might return at any moment. "And, after that?" he inquired.

"After that—well—M. Raymond recovered, and in about three months' time he was out again; but the parents, who were old folks, had received their death-blow. They never rallied from the shock. Perhaps they felt that it was their own hard-heartedness and obstinacy that had caused their daughter's ruin—and remorse is hard to bear. They waned perceptibly from day to day, and during the following year they were borne to the cemetery within two months of each other."

From the spurious clerk's demeanor it was easy to see that he had ceased thinking about his omnibus, and his hostess felt both reassured and flattered. "And Mademoiselle Hermine?" he inquired, eagerly.

"Alas! monsieur, no one ever knew where she went, or what became of her."

"Didn't they try to find her?"

"They searched for her everywhere, for I don't know how long; all the ablest detectives in France and in foreign countries tried to find her, but not one of them succeeded in discovering the slightest trace of her whereabouts. M. Raymond promised an enormous sum to the man who would find his sister's betrayer.

He wished to kill him, and he sought for him for
years; but all in vain."

"And did they never receive any tidings of this unfortunate girl?"

"I was told that they heard from her twice. On
the morning following her flight her parents received
a letter, in which she implored their forgiveness. Five
or six months later, she wrote again to say that she
knew her brother was not dead. She confessed that
she was a wicked, ungrateful girl—that she had been
mad; but she said that her punishment had come, and
it was terrible. She added that every link was severed
between herself and her friends, and she hoped they
would forget her as completely as if she had never
existed. She went so far as to say that her children
should never know who their mother was, and that
never in her life again would she utter the name which
she had so disgraced."

It was the old, sad story of a ruined girl paying for
a moment's madness with her happiness and all her
after life. A terrible drama, no doubt; but one that
is of such frequent occurrence that it seems as com-
monplace as life itself. Thus any one who was acquainted with M. Isidore Fortunat would have been
surprised to see how greatly he was moved by such a
trifle. "Poor girl!" said he, in view of saying something. And then, in a tone of assumed carelessness,
he inquired: "Did they never discover what scoundrel
carried Mademoiselle de Chalusse away?"

"Never. Who he was, whence he came, whether he
was young or old, how he became acquainted with
Mademoiselle Hermine—these questions were never
answered. It was rumored at one time that he was an
American, a captain in the navy; but that was only a

rumor. To tell the truth, they never even discovered his name."

"What, not even his name?"

"Not even his name."

Unable to master his emotion, M. Fortunat had at least the presence of mind to rise and step back into the darker part of the shop. But his gesture of disappointment and the muttered oath that fell from his lips did not escape Madame Vantrasson. She was startled, and from that moment she looked upon the supposed clerk with evident distrust. It was not long before he again resumed his seat nearer the counter, still a trifle pale, perhaps, but apparently calm. Two questions more seemed indispensable to him, and yet either one of them would be sure to arouse suspicion. Nevertheless, he resolved to incur the risk of betraying himself. And, after all, what would it matter now? Did he not possess the information he had wished for, at least as much of it as it was in this woman's power to impart? "I can scarcely tell you, my dear madame, how much your narrative has interested me," he began. "I can confess now that I am slightly acquainted with the Count de Chalusse, and that I have frequently visited the house in the Rue de Courcelles, where he now resides."

"You!" exclaimed the woman, taking a hasty inventory of M. Fortunat's toilette.

"Yes, I—on the part of my employer, understand. Each time I've been to visit M. de Chalusse's I've seen a young lady whom I took for his daughter there. I was wrong, no doubt, since he isn't a married man——"

He paused. Astonishment and anger seemed to be almost suffocating his hostess. Without understanding how or why, she felt convinced that she had been

duped; and if she had obeyed her first impulse she
would have attacked M. Isidore then and there. If
she restrained this impulse, if she made an effort to
control herself, it was only because she thought she
held a better revenge in reserve.

"A young lady in the count's house!" she said,
thoughtfully. "That's scarcely possible. I've never
seen her; I've never heard her spoken of. How long
has she been there?"

"For six or seven months?"

"In that case, I can't absolutely deny it. It's two
years since I set foot in the count's house."

"I fancied this young lady might be the count's niece
Mademoiselle Hermine's daughter."

Madame Vantrasson shook her head. "Put that
fancy out of your head," she remarked. "The count
said that his sister was dead to him from the evening
of her flight."

"Who *can* this young girl be, then?"

"Bless me! I don't know. What sort of a looking
person is she?"

"Very tall; a brunette."

"How old is she?"

"Eighteen or nineteen."

The woman made a rapid calculation on her fingers.
"Nine and four are thirteen," she muttered, "and five
are eighteen. Ah, ha!—why not? I must look into
this."

"What did you say?"

"Nothing; a little reflection I was making to myself.
Do you know this young lady's name?"

"It's Marguerite."

The woman's face clouded. "No; it can't be then,"
she muttered, in a scarcely audible voice.

M. Fortunat was on coals of fire. It was evident that this frightful creature, even if she knew nothing definite, had some idea, some vague suspicion of the truth. How could he compel her to speak now that she was on her guard? He had not time to ascertain, for the door suddenly opened, and Vantrasson appeared on the threshold. He was scarcely sober when he left the shop, but now he was fairly drunk; his heavy shamble had become a stagger. "Oh, you wretch, you brigand!" howled his wife; "you've been drinking again!"

He succeeded in maintaining his equilibrium, and, gazing at her with the phlegmatic stare peculiar to intoxicated men, he replied: "Well, what of that! Can't I have a little pleasure with my friends? I came across a couple of men who were just taking their fifteenth glass; why should I refuse a compliment?"

"You can't hold yourself up."

"That's true." And to prove it he tumbled on to a chair.

A torrent of abuse now flowed from Madame Vantrasson's lips! M. Fortunat only imperfectly distinguished the words "thief," "spy," and "detective;" but he could not mistake the meaning of the looks which she alternately gave her husband and himself. "It's a fortunate thing for you that my husband is in this condition," her glances plainly implied, "otherwise there would be an explanation, and then we should see——"

"I've had a lucky escape," thought the spurious clerk. But as matters stood there was nothing to fear. It was a case where one could show a brave front to the enemy without incurring the slightest danger. "Let your husband alone," said he. "If he has only brought

the paper that he was sent to fetch, I sha'n't have lost
my evening to oblige you."

Vantrasson had brought not one sheet of stamped
paper, but two. A bad pen and some muddy ink were
produced, and M. Fortunat began to draw up an acknowledgment according to the established formula.
However, it was necessary to mention the name of the
creditor of whom he had spoken, and not wishing to
state his own, he used that of poor Victor Chupin, who
was at that very moment shivering at the door, little
suspecting what liberty was being taken with his cog-
nomen.

"Chupin!" repeated the vixen, as if to engrave the
name on her memory; "Victor Chupin! I should
just like to see him," she added, viciously.

When the document was finished, it became necessary to wake Vantrasson, so that he might sign it. He
did so with very good grace, and his wife appended her
signature beside her husband's. Thereupon M. Fortunat gave them in exchange the note which had served
as a pretext for his visit. "And above all," he remarked, as he opened the door to go, "don't forget
that you are to pay something on account each month."

"Go to the devil, and your account with you!"
growled Madame Vantrasson.

But Fortunat did not hear this. He was already
walking down the road by the side of Chupin, who
was saying: "Well, here you are, at last, m'sieur! I
thought you had taken a lease of that old barrack. If
ever I come here again, I'll bring a foot-warmer with
me."

But one of those fits of profound abstraction to which
determined seekers after truth are subject had taken
possession of M. Fortunat, and made him oblivious of

all surrounding circumstances. His heart had been full of hope when he reached the Asnières Road, but he went away gloomy and despondent; and quite unconscious of the darkness, the mud, and the rain, which was again falling, he silently plodded along in the middle of the highway. Chupin was obliged to stop him at the city gate, and remind him that the cab was waiting.

"That's true," was M. Fortunat's only answer. He entered the vehicle, certainly without knowing it; and as they rolled homeward, the thoughts that filled his brain to overflowing found vent in a sort of monologue, of which Chupin now and then caught a few words. "What a piece of business!" he muttered—"what a piece of business! I've had seven years' experience in such matters, and yet I've never met with an affair so shrouded in mystery. My forty thousand francs are in a precarious condition. Certainly I've lost money before through heirs whose existence I hadn't even suspected; but by reinstating these same heirs in their rights, I've regained my lost money, and received a handsome reward in addition; but in this case all is darkness; there isn't a single gleam of light —not the slightest clew. If I could only find them! But how can I search for people whose names I don't even know—for people who have escaped all the inquiries of the police? And where shall I look for them —in Europe, in America? It would be sheer madness! To whom, then, will the count's millions go?"

It was only the sudden stoppage of the cab in front of his own door that recalled M. Fortunat to the realities of life. "Here are twenty francs, Victor," he said to Chupin. "Pay the driver, and keep the rest yourself."

As he spoke, he sprang nimbly to the ground. A handsome brougham, drawn by two horses, was standing before the house. "The Marquis de Valorsay's carriage," muttered M. Fortunat. "He has been very patient; he has waited for me—or, rather, he has waited for my ten thousand francs. Well, we shall see."

III.

M. FORTUNAT had scarcely started off on his visit to the Vantrassons when the Marquis de Valorsay reached the Place de la Bourse.

"Monsieur has gone out," said Madame Dodelin, as she opened the door.

"You must be mistaken, my good woman."

"No, no; my master said you would, perhaps, wait for him."

"Very well; I will do so."

Faithful to the orders she had received, the servant conducted the visitor to the drawing-room, lit the tapers in the candelabra, and retired. "This is very strange!" growled the marquis. "Monsieur Fortunat makes an appointment, Monsieur Fortunat expects me to wait for him! What will happen next?" However, he drew a newspaper from his pocket, threw himself into an arm-chair, and waited.

By his habits and tastes, the Marquis de Valorsay belonged to that section of the aristocracy which has coined the term "high life" in view of describing its own manners and customs. The matters that engrossed the marquis's frivolous mind were club-life and first performances at the opera and the leading theatres, social duties and visits to the fashionable watering-places, racing and the shooting and hunting seasons, together with his mistress and his tailor.

He considered that to ride in a steeple-chase was an act of prowess worthy of his ancestors; and when he galloped past the stand, clad as a jockey, in top-boots and a violet silk jacket, he believed he read admiration in every eye. This was his every-day life, which had been enlivened by a few salient episodes : two duels, an elopement with a married woman, a twenty-six hours' *séance* at the gaming table, and a fall from his horse, while hunting, which nearly cost him his life. These acts of valor had raised him considerably in the estimation of his friends, and procured him a celebrity of which he was not a little proud. The newspaper reporters were constantly mentioning his name, and the sporting journals never failed to chronicle his departure from Paris or his arrival in the city.

Unfortunately, such a life of busy idleness has its trials and its vicissitudes, and M. de Valorsay was a living proof of this. He was only thirty-three, but in spite of the care he expended upon his toilette, he looked at least forty. Wrinkles were beginning to show themselves; it required all the skill of his valet to conceal the bald spots on his cranium; and since his fall from his horse, he had been troubled by a slight stiffness in his right leg, which stiffness became perfect lameness in threatening weather. Premature lassitude pervaded his entire person, and when he relaxed in vigilance even his eyes betrayed a distaste for everything—weariness, satiety as it were. All the same, however, he bore himself with an undeniable air of distinction, albeit the haughtiness of his manner indicated an exaggerated idea of his own importance. He was indeed in the habit of treating all those whom

he considered his inferiors with supercilious suffi-
ciency.

The clock on M. Fortunat's mantel-shelf struck eleven
at last and the marquis rose to his feet with a muttered
oath. "This is too much!" he growled, angrily.

He looked about for a bell, and seeing none, he was
reduced to the dire necessity of opening the door himself, and calling some one. Madame Dodelin answered
the summons. "Monsieur said he would return before
midnight," she replied; "so he will certainly be here.
There is no one like him for punctuality. Won't monsieur have patience a little longer?"

"Well, I will wait a few moments; but, my good
woman, light the fire; my feet are frozen!"

M. Fortunat's drawing-room being used but seldom,
was really as frigid as an iceberg; and to make matters still worse, M. de Valorsay was in evening dress,
with only a light overcoat. The servant hesitated for
an instant, thinking this visitor difficult to please, and
inclined to make himself very much at home, still she
obeyed.

"I think I ought to go," muttered the marquis. "I
really think I ought to go." And yet he remained.
Necessity, it should be remembered, effectually quiets
the revolts of pride.

Left an orphan in his early childhood, placed in possession of an immense fortune at the age of twenty-
three, M. de Valorsay had entered life like a famished
man enters a dining-room. His name entitled him to
a high position in the social world; and he installed
himself at table without asking how much the banquet
might cost him. It cost him dear, as he discovered at
the end of the first year, on noting that his disburse-
ments had considerably exceeded his large income. It

was very evident that if he went on in this way, each twelvemonth would deepen an abyss where in the one hundred and sixty thousand francs a year, left him by his father, would finally be swallowed up. But he had plenty of time to reflect upon this unpleasant possibility ere it could come to pass! And, besides, he found his present life so delightful, and he obtained so much gratification for his money, that he was unwilling to make any change. He possessed several fine estates, and he found plenty of men who were only too glad to lend him money on such excellent security. He borrowed timidly at first, but more boldly when he discovered what a mere trifle a mortgage is. Moreover, his wants increased in proportion to his vanity. Occupying a certain position in the opinion of his acquaintances, he did not wish to descend from the heights to which they had exalted him; and the very fact that he had been foolishly extravagant one year made it necessary for him to be guilty of similar folly during the succeeding twelvemonth. He failed to pay his creditors the interest that was due on his loans. They did not ask him for it; and perhaps he forgot that it was slowly but surely accumulating, and that at the end of a certain number of years the amount of his indebtedness would be doubled. He never thought what the end would be. He became absolutely ignorant of the condition of his affairs, and really arrived at the conclusion that his resources were inexhaustible. He believed this until one day when on going to his lawyer for some money, that gentleman coldly said: "You requested me to obtain one hundred thousand francs for you, Monsieur le Marquis—but I have only been able to procure fifty thousand—here they are. And do not hope for more. All your real estate is encumbered

beyond its value. Your creditors will probably leave
you in undisturbed possession for another year—it will
be to their interest—but when it has elapsed they will
take possession of their own, as they have a perfect
right to do." Then, with a meaning smile, the smile
of a wily prime minister, he added: "If I were in your
place, Monsieur le Marquis, I would profit by this year
of grace. You undoubtedly understand what I mean.
I have the honor to wish you good-morning."

What an awakening—after a glorious dream that
had lasted for ten years. M. de Valorsay was stunned
—crushed. For three days he remained immured in his
own room, obstinately refusing to receive any one.
" The marquis is ill," was his valet's answer to every
visitor.

M. de Valorsay felt that he must have time to regain his mental equilibrium—to look his situation
calmly in the face. It was a frightful one, for his ruin
was complete, absolute. He could save nothing from
the wreck. What was to become of him? What could
he do? He set his wits to work; but he found that he
was incapable of plying any kind of avocation. All the
energy he had been endowed with by nature had been
squandered—exhausted in pandering to his self-conceit.
If he had been younger he might have turned soldier;
but at his age he had not even this resource. Then it
was that his notary's smile recurred to his mind. " His
advice was decidedly good," he muttered. " All is not
yet lost; one way of escape still remains—marriage."

And why, indeed, shouldn't he marry, and marry a
rich wife too? No one knew anything about his misfortune; for a year at least, he would retain all the
advantages that wealth bestows upon its possessor. His
name alone was a great advantage. It would be very

strange if he could not find some manufacturer's or banker's daughter who would be only too delighted to have a marquisial coronet emblazoned on her carriage panels.

Having arrived at this conclusion, M. de Valorsay began his search, and it was not long before he thought he had found what he was seeking. But something was still necessary. The bestowers of large dowers are inclined to be suspicious; they like to have a clear understanding as to the financial position of the suitors who present themselves, and they not unfrequently ask for information. Accordingly, before committing himself, M. de Valorsay understood that it was necessary he should provide himself with an intelligent and devoted adviser. There must be some one to hold his creditors in check, to silence them, and obtain sundry concessions from them—in a word, some one to interest them in his success. With this object in view, M. de Valorsay applied to his notary; but the latter utterly refused to mix himself up in any such affair, and declared that the marquis's suggestion was almost an insult. Then touched, perhaps, by his client's apparent despair, he said, " But I can mention a person who might be of service to you. Go to M. Isidore Fortunat, No. 27 Place de la Bourse. If you succeed in interesting him in your marriage, it is an accomplished fact."

It was under these circumstances that the marquis became acquainted with M. Fortunat. M. de Valorsay was a man of no little penetration, and on his first visit he carefully weighed his new acquaintance. He found him to be the very counsellor he desired—prudent, and at the same time courageous; fertile in expedients; a thorough master of the art of evading the law, and not at all troubled by scruples. With such an adviser, it would be mere child's play to conceal his financial embarrassments and deceive the most suspicious father-in-law. So M. de Valorsay did not hesitate a moment. He frankly disclosed his pecuniary condition and his matrimonial hopes, and concluded by promising M. Fortunat a certain percentage on the bride's dowry, to be paid on the day following the marriage.

After a prolonged conference, the agreement was drawn up and signed, and that very day M. Fortunat took the nobleman's interests in hand. How heartily, and with what confidence in his success, is shown by the fact that he had advanced forty thousand francs for his client's use, out of his own private purse. After such a proof of confidence the marquis could hardly have been dissatisfied with his adviser; in point of fact, he was delighted with him, and all the more so, as this invaluable man always treated him with extreme deference, verging on servility. And in M. de Valorsay's eyes this was a great consideration; for he was becoming more arrogant and more irascible in proportion as his right to be so diminished. Secretly disgusted with himself, and deeply humiliated by the shameful intrigue to which he had stooped, he took a secret satisfaction in crushing his accomplice with his imaginary superiority and lordly disdain. According as his humor was good or bad, he called him " my dear extortioner," " Mons. Fortunat," or " Master Twenty-per-cent." But though these sneers and insults drove the obsequious smile from M. Fortunat's lips, he was quite capable of including them in the bill under the head of sundries.

The unvarying deference and submission which M. de Valorsay's adviser displayed made his failure to keep the present appointment all the more remarkable.

Such neglect of the commonest rules of courtesy was inconceivable on the part of so polite a man; and the marquis's anger gradually changed to anxiety. "What can have happened?" he thought.

He was trying to decide whether he should leave or stay, when he heard a key grate in the lock of the outer door, and then some quick steps along the ante-room. "At last—here he is!" he muttered, with a sigh of relief.

He expected to see M. Fortunat enter the room at once, but he was disappointed. The agent had no desire to show himself in the garb which he had assumed for his excursion with Chupin; and so he had hastened to his room to don his wonted habiliments. He also desired a few moments for deliberation.

If—as was most probably the case—M. de Valorsay were ignorant of the Count de Chalusse's critical condition, was it advisable to tell him of it? M. Fortunat thought not, judging with reason that this would lead to a discussion and very possibly to a rupture, and he wished to avoid anything of the kind until he was quite certain of the count's death.

Meanwhile the marquis was thinking—he was a trifle late about it—that he had done wrong to wait in that drawing-room for three mortal hours. Was such conduct worthy of him? Had he shown himself proper respect? Would not M. Fortunat construe this as an acknowledgment of the importance of his services and his client's urgent need? Would he not become more exacting, more exorbitant in his demands? If the marquis could have made his escape unheard, he would, no doubt, have done so; but this was out of the question. So he resorted to a stratagem which seemed to him likely to save his compromised dignity.

He stretched himself out in his arm-chair, closed his
eyes, and pretended to doze. Then, when M. Fortunat
at last entered the drawing-room he sprang up as if he
were suddenly aroused from slumber, rubbed his eyes,
and exclaimed: "Eh! what's that? Upon my word I
must have been asleep!"

But M. Fortunat was not deceived. He noticed, on
the floor, a torn and crumpled newspaper, which betrayed the impatience and anger his client had experienced during his long waiting. "Well," resumed
the marquis, "what time is it? Half-past twelve?
This is a pretty time to keep an appointment fixed for
ten o'clock. This is presuming on my good-nature, M.
Fortunat! Do you know that my carriage has been
waiting below ever since half-past nine, and that my
horses have, perhaps, taken cold? A pair of horses
worth six hundred louis!"

M. Fortunat listened to these reproaches with the
deepest humility. "You must excuse me, Monsieur
le Marquis," said he. "If I remained out so much
later than usual, it was only because your business interests detained me."

"Zounds! that is about the same as if it had been
your own business that detained you!" And well
pleased with this joke, he added, "Ah well! How
are affairs progressing?"

"On my side as well as could be desired."

The marquis had resumed his seat in the chimney-
corner, and was poking the fire with a haughty, but
poorly assumed air of indifference. "I am listening,"
he said carelessly.

"In that case, Monsieur le Marquis, I will state the
facts in a few words, without going into particulars.
Thanks to an expedient devised by me, we shall obtain

for twenty hours a release from all the mortgages that
now encumber your estates. On that very day we will
request a certificate from the recorder. This certificate
will declare that your estates are free from all encum-
brances; you will show this statement to M. de Chalusse, and all his doubts—that is, if he has any—will
vanish. The plan was very simple; the only difficulty
was about raising the money, but I have succeeded in
doing so. All your creditors but two lent themselves
very readily to the arrangement. I have now won the
consent of the two who at first refused, but we shall
have to pay dearly for it. It will cost you about twenty-
six thousand francs."

M. de Valorsay was so delighted that he could not
refrain from clapping his hands. "Then the affair is
virtually concluded," he exclaimed. "In less than a
month Mademoiselle Marguerite will be the Marquise
de Valorsay, and I shall have a hundred thousand
francs a year again." Then, noting how gravely M.
Fortunat shook his head: "Ah! so you doubt it!" he
cried. "Very well; now it is your turn to listen. Yesterday I had a long conference with the Count de
Chalusse, and everything has been settled. We exchanged our word of honor, Master Twenty-per-cent.
The count does things in a princely fashion; he gives
Mademoiselle Marguerite two millions."

"Two millions!" the other repeated like an echo.

"Yes, my dear miser, neither more nor less. Only
for private reasons, which he did not explain, the count
stipulates that only two hundred thousand francs shall
appear in the marriage contract. The remaining eighteen hundred thousand francs, he gives to me unre-
servedly and unconditionally. Upon my word, I think
this very charming. How does it strike you?"

M. Fortunat made no reply. M. de Valorsay's gayety, instead of cheering, saddened him. "Ah! my fine fellow," he thought, "you would sing a different song if you knew that by this time M. de Chalusse is probably dead, and that most likely Mademoiselle Marguerite has only her beautiful eyes left her, and will dim them in weeping for her vanished millions."

But this brilliant scion of the aristocracy had no suspicion of the real state of affairs, for he continued: "You will say, perhaps, it is strange, that I, Ange-Marie Robert Dalbou, Marquis de Valorsay, should marry a girl whose father and mother no one knows, and whose only name is Marguerite. In this respect it is true that the match is not exactly a brilliant one. Still, as it will appear that she merely has a fortune of two hundred thousand francs, no one will accuse me of marrying for money on the strength of my name. On the contrary, it will seem to be a love-match, and people will suppose that I have grown young again." He paused, incensed by M. Fortunat's lack of enthusiasm. "Judging from your long face, Master Twenty-per-cent, one would fancy you doubted my success," he said.

"It is always best to doubt," replied his adviser, philosophically.

The marquis shrugged his shoulders. "Even when one has triumphed over all obstacles?" he asked sneeringly.

"Yes."

"Then, tell me, if you please, what prevents this marriage from being a foregone conclusion?"

"Mademoiselle Marguerite's consent, Monsieur le Marquis."

It was as if a glass of ice-water had been thrown in

M. de Valorsay's face. He started, turned as pale as
death, and then exclaimed: "I shall have that; I am
sure of it."

You could not say that M. Fortunat was angry.
Such a man, as cold and as smooth as a hundred franc
piece, has no useless passions. But he was intensely
irritated to hear his client foolishly chanting the pæons
of victory, while he was compelled to conceal his grief
at the loss of his forty thousand francs, deep in the
recesses of his heart. So, far from being touched by
the marquis's evident alarm, it pleased him to be able
to turn the dagger in the wound he had just inflicted.
"You must excuse my incredulity," said he. "It
comes entirely from something you, yourself, told me
about a week ago."

"What did I tell you?"

"That you suspected Mademoiselle Marguerite of
a—how shall I express it?—of a secret preference for
some other person."

The gloomiest despondency had now followed the
marquis's enthusiasm and exultation. He was evidently in torture. "I more than suspected it," said he.

"Ah!"

"I was certain of it, thanks to the count's housekeeper, Madame Léon, a miserable old woman whom
I have hired to look after my interests. She has been
watching Mademoiselle Marguerite, and saw a letter
written by her——"

"Oh!"

"Certainly nothing has passed that Mademoiselle
Marguerite has any cause to blush for. The letter,
which is now in my possession, contains unmistakable
proofs of that. She might proudly avow the love she has
inspired, and which she undoubtedly returns. Yet——"

M. Fortunat's gaze was so intent that it became unbearable. "You see, then," he began, "that I had good cause to fear——"

Exasperated beyond endurance, M. de Valorsay sprang up so violently that he overturned his chair. "No!" he exclaimed, "no, a thousand times no! You are wrong—for the man who loves Mademoiselle Marguerite is now ruined. Yes, such is really the case. While we are sitting here, at this very moment, he is lost—irredeemably lost. Between him and the woman whom I wish to marry—whom I *shall* marry—I have dug so broad and deep an abyss that the strongest love cannot overleap it. It is better and worse than if I had killed him. Dead, he would have been mourned, perhaps; while now, the lowest and most degraded woman would turn from him in disgust, or, even if she loved him, she would not dare to confess it."

M. Fortunat seemed greatly disturbed. "Have you then put into execution the project—the plan you spoke of?" he faltered. "I thought you were only jesting."

The marquis lowered his head. "Yes," he answered.

His companion stood for a moment as if petrified, and then suddenly exclaimed: "What! You have done that—you—a gentleman?"

M. de Valorsay paced the floor in a state of intense agitation. Had he caught a glimpse of his own face in the looking-glass, it would have frightened him. "A gentleman!" he repeated, in a tone of suppressed rage; "a gentleman! That word is in everybody's mouth, nowadays. Pray, what do you understand by a gentleman, Mons. Fortunat? No doubt, you mean a heroic idiot who passed through life with a lofty mien, clad in all the virtues, as stoical as Job, and as resigned as a martyr—a sort of moral Don Quixote, preaching the austerest virtue, and practising it? But, unfortunately, nobility of soul and of purpose are expensive luxuries, and I am a ruined man. I am no saint! I love life and all that makes life beautiful and desirable—and to procure its pleasures I must fight with the weapons of the age. No doubt, it is grand to be honest; but in my case it is so impossible, that I prefer to be dishonest—to commit an act of shameful infamy which will yield a hundred thousand francs a year. This man is in my way—I suppress him—so much the worse for him—he has no business to be in my way. If I could have met him openly, I would have dispatched him according to the accepted code of honor; but, then, I should have had to renounce all idea of marrying Mademoiselle Marguerite, so I was obliged to find some other way. I could not choose my means. The drowning man does not reject the plank, which is his only chance of salvation, because it chances to be dirty."

His gestures were even more forcible than his words; and when he concluded, he threw himself on to the sofa, holding his head tightly between his hands, as if he felt that it was bursting. Anger choked his utterance—not anger so much as something he would not confess, the quickening of his own conscience and the revolt of every honorable instinct; for, in spite of his sins of omission, and of commission, never, until this day, had he actually violated any clause of the code acknowledged by men of honor.

"You have been guilty of a most infamous act, Monsieur le Marquis," said M. Fortunat, coldly.

"Oh! no moralizing, if you please."

"Only evil will come of it."

The marquis shrugged his shoulders, and in a tone of

bitter scorn, retorted: "Come, Mons. Fortunat, if you wish to lose the forty thousand francs you advanced to me, it's easy enough to do so. Run to Madame d'Argelés's house, ask for M. de Coralth, and tell him I countermand my order. My rival will be saved, and will marry Mademoiselle Marguerite and her millions."

M. Fortunat remained silent. He could not tell the marquis: "My forty thousand francs are lost already. I know that only too well. Mademoiselle Marguerite is no longer the possessor of millions, and you have committed a useless crime." However, it was this conviction which imparted such an accent of eagerness to his words as he continued to plead the cause of virtue and of honesty. Would he have said as much if he had entertained any great hope of the success of the marquis's matrimonial enterprise? It is doubtful, still we must do M. Fortunat the justice to admit that he was really and sincerely horrified by what he had unhesitatingly styled an "infamous act."

The marquis listened to his agent for a few moments in silence, and then rose to his feet again. "All this is very true," he interrupted; "but I am, nevertheless, anxious to learn the result of my little plot. For this reason, Monsieur Fortunat, give me at once the five hundred louis you promised me, and I will then bid you good-evening."

The agent had been preparing himself for this moment, and yet he trembled. "I am deeply grieved, monsieur," he replied, with a doleful smile; "it was this matter that kept me out so much later than usual this evening. I hoped to have obtained the money from a banker, who has always accommodated me before— M. Prosper Bertomy, you know him: he married M. André Fauvel's niece——"

"Yes, I know; proceed, if you please."

" Ah, well! it was impossible for me to procure the money."

The marquis had hitherto been pale, but now his face flushed crimson. " This is a jest, I suppose," said he.

" Alas!—unfortunately—no."

There was a moment's silence, which the marquis probably spent in reflecting upon the probable consequences of this disappointment, for it was in an almost threatening tone that he eventually exclaimed: " You know that I must have this money at once— that I *must* have it."

M. Fortunat would certainly have preferred to lose a good pound of flesh rather than the sum of money mentioned; but, on the other hand, he felt that it would not do for him to sever his connection with his client until the death of the Count de Chalusse was certain; and being anxious to save his money and to keep his client, his embarrassment was extreme. " It was the most unfortunate thing in the world," he stammered; " I apprehended no difficulty whatever—" Then, suddenly clapping his hand to his forehead, he exclaimed: " But, Monsieur le Marquis, couldn't you borrow this amount from one of your friends, the Duke de Champdoce or the Count de Commarin?—that would be a good idea."

M. de Valorsay was anything but unsophisticated, and his natural shrewdness had been rendered much more acute by the difficulties with which he had recently been obliged to contend. M. Fortunat's confusion had not escaped his keen glance; and this last suggestion aroused his suspicions at once. " What!" he said, slowly, and with an air of evident distrust

"*You* give me this advice, Master Twenty-per-cent.
This is wonderful! How long is it since your opinions
have undergone such a change?"

"My opinions?"

"Yes. Didn't you say to me during our first interview; 'The thing that will save you, is that you have
never in your while life borrowed a louis from a friend.
An ordinary creditor only thinks of a large interest;
and if that is paid him he holds his peace. A friend
is never satisfied until everybody knows that he has
generously obliged you. It is far better to apply to a
usurer.' I thought all that very sensible, and I quite
agreed with you when you added: 'So, Monsieur le
Marquis, no borrowing of this kind until after your
marriage—not on any pretext whatever. Go without
eating rather than do it. Your credit is still good; but
it is being slowly undermined—and the indiscretion of
a friend who chanced to say: "I think Valorsay is hard
up," might fire the train, and then you'd explode.'"

M. Fortunat's embarrassment was really painful to
witness. He was not usually wanting in courage, but
the events of the evening had shaken his confidence and
his composure. The hope of gain and the fear of loss
had deprived him of his wonted clearness of mind.
Feeling that he had just committed a terrible blunder,
he racked his brain to find some way of repairing it,
and finding none, his confusion increased.

"Did you, or didn't you, use that language?" insisted M. de Valorsay. "What have you to say in
reply?"

"Circumstances——"

"What circumstances?"

"Urgent need—necessity. There is no rule without
its exceptions. I did not imagine you would be so

rash. I have advanced you forty thousand francs in less than five months—it is outrageous. If I were in your place, I would be more reasonable—I would economize——"

He paused! in fact, he was compelled to pause by the piercing glance which M. de Valorsay turned upon him. He was furious with himself. " I am losing my wits," he thought.

" Still more wise counsel," remarked the ruined nobleman ironically. " While you are about it, why don't you advise me to sell my horses and carriages, and establish myself in a garret in the Rue Amelot? Such a course would seem very natural, wouldn't it? and, of course, it would inspire M. de Chalusse with boundless confidence! "

" But without going to such extremes——"

" Hold your tongue! " interrupted the marquis, violently. " Better than any one else you know that I cannot retrench, although the reality no longer exists. I am condemned, cost what it may, to keep up appearances. That is my only hope of salvation. I have gambled, given expensive suppers, indulged in dissipation of every kind, and I must continue to do so. I have come to hate Ninette Simplon, for whom I have committed so many acts of folly, and yet I still keep her—to show that I am rolling in wealth. I have thrown thousand-franc notes out of the window, and I mustn't stop throwing them. Indeed, what would people say if I stopped! Why, 'Valorsay is a ruined man!' Then, farewell to my hopes of marrying an heiress. And so I am always gay and smiling; that is part of my *rôle*. What would my servants—the twenty spies that I pay—what would they think if they saw me thoughtful or disturbed? You would scarcely believe it, M. Fortunat, but I have positively been reduced to dining on credit at my club, because I had paid, that morning, for a month's provender for my horses! It is true I have many valuable articles in my house, but I cannot dispose of them. People would recognize them at once; besides, they form a part of my stock-in-trade. An actor doesn't sell his costumes because he's hungry—he goes without food—and when it's time for the curtain to rise, he dons his satin and velvet garments, and, despite his empty stomach, he chants the praises of a bountiful table and rare old wine. That is what I am doing—I, Robert Dalbou, Marquis de Valorsay! At the races at Vincennes, about a fortnight ago, I was bowling along the boulevard behind my four-in-hand, when I heard a laborer say, 'How happy those rich people must be!' Happy, indeed! Why, I envied him his lot. He was sure that the morrow would be like the day that preceded it. On that occasion my entire fortune consisted of a single louis, which I had won at baccarat the evening before. As I entered the enclosure, Isabelle, the flower-girl, handed me a rose for my button-hole. I gave her my louis—but I longed to strangle her!"

He paused for a moment, and then, in a frenzy of passion, he advanced toward M. Fortunat, who instinctively retreated into the protecting embrasure of a window. "And for eight months I have lived this horrible life!" he resumed. "For eight months each moment has been so much torture. Ah! better poverty, prison, and shame! And now, when the prize is almost won, actuated either by treason or caprice, you try to make all my toil and all my suffering unavailing. You try to thwart me on the very threshold of success! No! I swear, by God's sacred name, it shall not be! I will rather crush you, you miserable scoundrel—crush you like a venomous reptile!"

There was such a ring of fury in his voice that the crystals of the candelabra vibrated; and Madame Dodelin, in her kitchen, heard it, and shuddered. "Some one will certainly do M. Fortunat an injury one of these days," she thought.

It was not by any means the first time that M. Fortunat had found himself at variance with clients of a sanguine temperament; but he had always escaped safe and sound, so that, after all, he was not particularly alarmed in the present instance, as was proved by the fact that he was still calm enough to reflect and plan. "In forty-eight hours I shall be certain of the count's fate," he thought; "he will be dead, or he will be in a fair way to recovery—so by promising to give this frenzied man what he desires on the day after to-morrow, I shall incur no risk."

Taking advantage of an opportunity which M. de Valorsay furnished, on pausing to draw breath, he hastily exclaimed, "Really, Monsieur le Marquis, I cannot understand your anger."

"What! scoundrel!"

"Excuse me. Before insulting me, permit me to explain——"

"No explanation—five hundred louis!"

"Have the kindness to allow me to finish. Yes, I know that you are in urgent need of money—not by-and-by, but now. To-day I was unable to procure it, nor can I promise it to-morrow; but on the day after to-morrow, Saturday, I shall certainly have it ready for you."

The marquis seemed to be trying to read his agent's very soul. "Are you in earnest?" he asked. "Show your hand. If you don't intend to help me out of my embarrassment, say so."

" Ah, Monsieur le Marquis, am I not as much interested in your success as you yourself can be? Have you not received abundant proofs of my devotion? "

" Then I can rely upon you."

" Absolutely." And seeing a lingering doubt in his client's eyes, M. Fortunat added, " You have my word of honor ! "

The clock struck three. The marquis took his hat and started toward the door. But M. Fortunat, in whose heart the word scoundrel was still rankling, stopped him. " Are you going to that lady's house now? What is she called? I've forgotten her name. Ah, yes, I remember now. Madame d'Argelès, isn't she called? It's at her place, I believe, that the reputation of Mademoiselle Marguerite's favored lover is to be ruined."

The marquis turned angrily. " What do you take me for, Master Twenty-per-cent? " he rudely asked. " That is one of those things no well-bred gentleman will do himself. But in Paris people can be found to do any kind of dirty work, if you are willing to pay them for it."

" Then how will you know the result? "

" Why, twenty minutes after the affair is over, M. de Coralth will be at my house. He is there even now, perhaps." And as this subject was anything but pleasant, he hastened away, exclaiming, " Get to bed, my dear extortioner. *Au revoir*. And, above all, remember your promise."

" My respects, Monsieur le Marquis."

But when the door closed, M. Fortunat's expression immediately changed. " Ah! you insult me ! " he muttered sullenly. "You rob me, and you call me a scoundrel into the bargain. You shall pay dearly for it, my fine fellow, no matter what may happen!"

IV.

IT is in vain that the law has endeavored to shield private life from prying eyes. The scribes who pander to Parisian curiosity surmount all obstacles and brave every danger. Thanks to the "High Life" reporters, every newspaper reader is aware that twice a week —Mondays and Thursdays—Madame Lia d'Argelès holds a reception at her charming mansion in the Rue de Berry. Her guests find plenty of amusement there. They seldom dance; but card-playing begins at midnight, and a dainty supper is served before the departure of the guests.

It was on leaving one of these little entertainments that that unfortunate young man, Jules Chazel, a cashier in a large banking-house, committed suicide by blowing out his brains. The brilliant frequenters of Madame d'Argelès's entertainments considered this act proof of exceeding bad taste and deplorable weakness on his part. "The fellow was a coward," they declared. "Why, he had lost hardly a thousand louis!"

He had lost only that, it is true—a mere trifle as times go. Only the money was not his; he had taken it from the safe which was confided to his keeping, expecting, probably, to double the amount in a single night. In the morning, when he found himself alone, without a penny, and the deficit staring him in the face, the voice of conscience cried, "You are a thief!" and he lost his reason.

The event created a great sensation at the time, and

the *Petit Journal* published a curious story concerning
this unfortunate young man's mother. The poor woman
—she was a widow—sold all she possessed, even the
bed on which she slept, and when she had succeeded in
gathering together twenty thousand francs—the ransom
of her son's honor—she carried them to the banker by
whom her boy had been employed. He took them,
without even asking the mother if she had enough left
to purchase her dinner that evening; and the fine gentleman, who had won and pocketed Jules Chazel's stolen
gold, thought the banker's conduct perfectly natural
and just. It is true that Madame d'Argelès was in despair during forty-eight hours or so; for the police
had begun a sort of investigation, and she feared this
might frighten her visitors and empty her drawing-
rooms. Not at all, however; on the contrary, she had
good cause to congratulate herself upon the notoriety
she gained through this suicide. For five days she was
the talk of Paris, and Alfred d'Aunay even published
her portrait in the *Illustrated Chronicle.*

Still, no one was able to say exactly who Madame
Lia d'Argelès was. Who was she, and whence did she
come? How had she lived until she sprang up, full
grown, in the sunshine of the fashionable world? Did
the splendid mansion in the Rue de Berry really belong to her? Was she as rich as she was supposed to
be? Where had she acquired such manners, the manners of a thorough woman of the world, with her many
accomplishments, as well as her remarkable skill as a
musician? Everything connected with her was a subject of conjecture, even to the name inscribed upon her
visiting cards—" Lia d'Argelès."

But no matter. Her house was always filled to overflowing; and at the very moment when the Marquis de

Valorsay and M. Fortunat were speaking of her, a dozen coroneted carriages stood before her door, and her rooms were thronged with guests. It was a little past midnight, and the bi-weekly card party had just been made up, when a footman announced, "Monsieur le Vicomte de Coralth! Monsieur Pascal Ferailleur!"

Few of the players deigned to raise their heads. But one man growled, "Good—two more players!" And four or five young men exclaimed, "Ah! here's Ferdinand! Good evening, my dear fellow!"

M. de Coralth was very young and remarkably good-looking, almost too good-looking, indeed; for his handsomeness was somewhat startling and unnatural. He had an exceedingly fair complexion, and large, melting black eyes, while a woman might have envied him his wavy brown hair and the exquisite delicacy of his skin. He dressed with great care and taste, and even coquettishly; his turn-down collar left his firm white throat uncovered, and his rose-tinted gloves fitted as perfectly as the skin upon his soft, delicate hands. He bowed familiarly on entering, and with a rather complacent smile on his lips, he approached Madame d'Argelès, who, half reclining in an easy chair near the fire-place, was conversing with two elderly gentlemen of grave and distinguished bearing. "How late you are, viscount," she remarked carelessly. "What have you been doing to-day? I fancied I saw you in the Bois, in the Marquis de Valorsay's dog-cart."

A slight flush suffused M. de Coralth's cheeks, and to hide it, perhaps, he turned toward the visitor who had entered with him, and drew him toward Madame d'Argelès, saying, "Allow me, madame, to present to you one of my great friends, M. Pascal Ferailleur, an

advocate whose name will be known to fame some
day."

"Your friends are always welcome at my house, my
dear viscount," replied Madame d'Argelès. And before Pascal had concluded his bow, she averted her
head, and resumed her interrupted conversation.

The new-comer, however, was worthy of more than
that cursory notice. He was a young man of five or
six-and-twenty, dark-complexioned and tall; each movement of his person was imbued with that natural grace
which is the result of perfect harmony of the muscles,
and of more than common vigor. His features were
irregular, but they gave evidence of energy, kindness
of heart, and honesty of purpose. A man possessing
such a proud, intelligent, and open brow, such a clear,
straightforward gaze, and such finely-cut lips, could be
no ordinary one. Deserted by his sponsor, who was
shaking hands right and left, he seated himself on a
sofa a little in the background; not because he was
embarrassed, but because he felt that instinctive distrust of self which frequently seizes hold of a person
on entering a crowd of strangers. He did his best to
conceal his curiosity, but nevertheless he looked and
listened with all his might.

The *salon* was an immense apartment, divided into
two rooms by sliding doors and hangings. When
Madame d'Argelès gave a ball, the rooms were thrown
into one; but, as a general rule, one room was occupied
by the card-players, and the other served as a refuge
for those who wished to chat. The card-room, into
which Pascal had been ushered, was an apartment of
noble proportions, furnished in a style of tasteful mag-
nificence. The tints of the carpet were subdued; there
was not too much gilding on the cornices; the clock

upon the mantel-shelf was chaste and elegant in design. The only thing at all peculiar about the room
and its appointments was a reflector, ingeniously arranged above the chandelier in such a way as to throw
the full glare of the candles upon the card-table which
stood directly beneath it. The table itself was adorned
with a rich tapestry cover, but this was visible only
at the corners, for it was covered, in turn, with a green
baize cloth considerably the worse for wear. Madame
d'Argelès's guests were probably not over fifty in number, but they all seemed to belong to the very best
society. The majority of them were men of forty
or thereabouts; several wore decorations, and two or
three of the eldest were treated with marked deference.
Certain well-known names which Pascal overheard surprised him greatly. " What! these men here? " he said
to himself; " and I—I regarded my visit as a sort of
clandestine frolic."

There were only seven or eight ladies present, none
of them being especially attractive. Their toilettes
were very costly, but in rather doubtful taste, and they
wore a profusion of diamonds. Pascal noticed that
these ladies were treated with perfect indifference, and
that, whenever the gentlemen spoke to them, they assumed an air of politeness which was too exaggerated
not to be ironical.

A score of persons were seated at the card-table, and
the guests who had retired into the adjoining *salon*
were silently watching the progress of the game, or
quietly chatting in the corners of the room. It surprised him to note that every one spoke in very low
tones; there was something very like respect, even awe,
in this subdued murmur. One might have supposed
that those present were celebrating the rites of some

mysterious worship. And is not gaming a species of
idolatry, symbolized by cards, and which has its
images, its fetishes, its miracles, its fanatics, and its
martyrs?

Occasionally, above the accompaniment of whispers,
rose the strange and incoherent exclamations of the
players: " Here are twenty louis! I take it—I pass!
The play is made! *Banco!*"

" What a strange gathering!" thought Pascal Ferailleur. " What singular people!" And he turned his
attention to the mistress of the house, as if he hoped to
decipher the solution of the enigma on her face.

But Madame Lia d'Argelès defied all analysis. She
was one of those women whose uncertain age varies
according to their mood, between the thirties and the
fifties; one who did not look over thirty in the evening,
but who would have been charged with being more
than fifty the next morning. In her youth she must
have been very beautiful, and she was still good-looking, though she had grown somewhat stout, and her
face had become a trifle heavy, thus marring the sym-
metry of her very delicate features. A perfect blonde,
she had eyes of so clear a blue that they seemed almost
faded. The whiteness of her skin was so unnatural
that it almost startled one. It was the dull, lifeless
white which suggests an excessive use of cosmetics and
rice powder, and long baths, late hours, and sleep at
day-time, in a darkened room. Her face was utterly
devoid of expression. One might have fancied that its
muscles had become relaxed after terrible efforts to
feign or to conceal some violent emotions; and there
was something melancholy, almost terrifying in the
eternal, and perhaps involuntary smile, which curved
her lips. She wore a dress of black velvet, with

slashed sleeves and bodice, a new design of the famous
man-milliner, Van Klopen.

Pascal was engaged in these observations when M. de
Coralth, having made his round, came and sat down
on the sofa beside him. "Well, what do you think of
it?" he inquired.

"Upon my word!" replied the young advocate, "I
am infinitely obliged to you for inviting me to accompany you here. I am intensely amused."

"Good! My philosopher is captivated."

"Not captivated, but interested, I confess." Then,
in the tone of good-humor which was habitual to him,
he added: "As for being the sage you call me, that's
all nonsense. And to prove it, I'm going to risk my
louis with the rest."

M. de Coralth seemed amazed, but a close observer
might have detected a gleam of triumph in his eyes.
"You are going to play—you?"

"Yes. Why not?"

"Take care!"

"Of what, pray? The worst I can do is to lose what
I have in my pocket—something over two hundred
francs."

The viscount shook his head thoughtfully. "It isn't
that which one has cause to fear. The devil always has
a hand in this business, and the first time a man plays
he's sure to win."

"And is that a misfortune?"

"Yes, because the recollection of these first winnings
is sure to lure you back to the gaming-table again.
You go back, you lose, you try to recover your money,
and that's the end of it—you become a gambler."

Pascal Ferailleur's smile was the smile of a man
who has full confidence in himself. "My brain is not

so easily turned, I hope," said he. " I have the thought of my name, and the fortune I must make, as ballast for it."

" I beseech you not to play," insisted the viscount. " Listen to me; you don't know what this passion for play is; the strongest and the coldest natures succumb —don't play."

He had raised his voice, as if he intended to be overheard by two guests who had just approached the sofa. They did indeed hear him. " Can I believe my own eyes and ears!" exclaimed one of them, an elderly man. " Can this really be Ferdinand who is trying to shake the allegiance of the votaries of our noble lady —the Queen of Spades?"

M. de Coralth turned quickly round: " Yes, it is indeed I," he answered. " I have purchased with my patrimony the right of saying: ' Distrust yourself, and don't do as I've done,' to an inexperienced friend."

The wisest counsels, given in a certain fashion, never fail to produce an effect diametrically opposed to that which they seemingly aim at. M. de Coralth's persistence, and the importance he attached to a mere trifle, could not fail to annoy the most patient man in the world, and in fact his patronizing tone really irritated Pascal. " You are free, my friend, to do as you please," said he; " but I——"

" Are you resolved?" interrupted the viscount.

" Absolutely."

" So be it, then. You are no longer a child, and I have warned you. Let us play, then." Thereupon they approached the table; room was made for them, and they seated themselves, Pascal being on M. Ferdinand de Coralth's right-hand side.

The guests were playing " Baccarat tournant," a

game of terrible and infantile simplicity. There are no
such things as skill or combination possible in it;
science and calculation are useless. Chance alone decides, and decides with the rapidity of lightning. Ama-
teurs certainly assert that, with great coolness and long
practice, one can, in a measure at least, avert prolonged
ill-luck. Maybe they are right, but it is not conclusively proved. Each person takes the cards in his
turn, risks what he chooses, and when his stakes are
covered, deals. If he wins, he is free to follow up his
vein of good-luck, or to pass the deal. When he loses,
the deal passes at once to the next player on the right.

A moment sufficed for Pascal Ferailleur to learn the
rules of the game. It was already Ferdinand's deal.
M. de Coralth staked a hundred francs; the bet was
taken; he dealt, lost, and handed the cards to Pascal.

The play, which had been rather timid at first—since
it was necessary, as they say, to try the luck—had
now become bolder. Several players had large piles
of gold before them, and the heavy artillery—that is
to say, bank-notes—were beginning to put in appearance. But Pascal had no false pride. " I stake a
louis! " said he.

The smallness of the sum attracted instant attention,
and two or three voices replied: " Taken! "

He dealt, and won. " Two louis! " he said again.
This wager was also taken; he won, and his run of luck
was so remarkable that, in a wonderfully short space
of time, he won six hundred francs.

" Pass the deal," whispered Ferdinand, and Pascal
followed this advice. " Not because I desire to keep
my winnings," he whispered in M. de Coralth's ear,
" but because I wish to have enough to play until the
end of the evening without risking anything."

But such prudence was unnecessary so far as he was concerned. When the deal came to him again, fortune favored him even more than before. He started with a hundred francs, and doubling them each time in six successive deals, he won more than three thousand francs.

"The devil! Monsieur is in luck."—"Zounds! And he is playing for the first time."—"That accounts for it. The inexperienced always win."

Pascal could not fail to hear these comments. The blood mantled over his cheeks, and, conscious that he was flushing, he, as usually happens, flushed still more. His good fortune embarrassed him, as was evident, and he played most recklessly. Still his good luck did not desert him; and do what he would he won—won continually. In fact, by four o'clock in the morning he had thirty-five thousand francs before him.

For some time he had been the object of close attention. "Do you know this gentleman?" inquired one of the guests.

"No. He came with Coralth."

"He is an advocate, I understand."

And all these whispered doubts and suspicions, these questions fraught with an evil significance, these uncharitable replies, grew into a malevolent murmur, which resounded in Pascal's ears and bewildered him. He was really becoming most uncomfortable, when Madame d'Argelès approached the card-table and exclaimed: "This is the third time, gentlemen, that you have been told that supper is ready. What gentleman will offer me his arm?"

There was an evident unwillingness to leave the table, but an old gentleman who had been losing heavily rose to his feet. "Yes, let us go to supper!" he exclaimed; "perhaps that will change the luck."

This was a decisive consideration. The room emptied as if by magic; and no one was left at the table but Pascal, who scarcely knew what to do with all the gold piled up before him. He succeeded, however, in distributing it in his pockets, and was about to join the other guests in the dining-room, when Madame d'Argelès abruptly barred his passage.

"I desire a word with you, monsieur," she said. Her face still retained its strange immobility, and the same stereotyped smile played about her lips. And yet her agitation was so evident that Pascal, in spite of his own uneasiness, noticed it, and was astonished by it.

"I am at your service, madame," he stammered, bowing.

She at once took his arm, and led him to the embrasure of a window. "I am a stranger to you, monsieur," she said, very hurriedly, and in very low tones, "and yet I must ask, and you must grant me, a great favor."

"Speak, madame."

She hesitated, as if at a loss for words, and then all of a sudden she said, eagerly: "You will leave this house at once, without warning any one, and while the other guests are at supper."

Pascal's astonishment changed into stupor.

"Why am I to go?" he asked.

"Because—but, no; I cannot tell you. Consider it only a caprice on my part—it is so; but I entreat you, don't refuse me. Do me this favor, and I shall be eternally grateful."

There was such an agony of supplication in her voice and her attitude, that Pascal was touched. A vague presentiment of some terrible, irreparable misfortune disturbed his own heart. Nevertheless, he sadly shook his head, and bitterly exclaimed: "You are, perhaps, not aware that I have just won over thirty thousand francs."

"Yes, I am aware of it. And this is only another, and still stronger reason why you should protect yourself against possible loss. It is well to pattern after Charlemagne* in this house. The other night, the Count d'Antas quietly made his escape bareheaded. He took a thousand louis away with him, and left his hat in exchange. The count is a brave man; and far from indulging in blame, every one applauded him the next day. Come, you have decided, I see—you will go; and to be still more safe, I will show you out through the servants' hall, then no one can possibly see you."

Pascal had almost decided to yield to her entreaties; but this proposed retreat through the back-door was too revolting to his pride to be thought of for a moment. "I will never consent to such a thing," he declared. "What would they think of me? Besides I owe them their revenge and I shall give it to them."

Neither Madame d'Argelès nor Pascal had noticed M. de Coralth, who in the meantime had stolen into the room on tiptoe, and had been listening to their conversation, concealed behind the folds of a heavy curtain. He now suddenly revealed his presence. "Ah! my dear friend," he exclaimed, in a winning tone. "While I honor your scruples, I must say that I think madame is a hundred times right. If I were in your

*French gamblers use this expression which they explain by the fact that Charlemagne departed this life with all his possessions intact, having always added to his dominions without ever experiencing a loss. Historically this is no doubt incorrect, but none the less, the expression prevails in France.—[TRANS.]

place, if I had won what you have won, I shouldn't hesitate. Others might think what they pleased; you have the money, that is the main thing."

For the second time, the viscount's intervention decided Pascal. "I shall remain," he said, resolutely.

But Madame d'Argelès laid her hand imploringly on his arm. "I entreat you, monsieur," said she. "Go now, there is still time——"

"Yes, go," said the viscount, approvingly, "it would be a most excellent move. Retreat and save the cash."

These words were like the drop which makes the cup overflow. Crimson with anger and assailed by the strangest suspicions, Pascal turned from Madame d'Argelès and hastened into the dining-room. The conversation ceased entirely on his arrival there. He could not fail to understand that he had been the subject of it. A secret instinct warned him that all the men around him were his enemies—though he knew not why—and that they were plotting against him. He also perceived that his slightest movements were watched and commented upon. However he was a brave man; his conscience did not reproach him in the least, and he was one of those persons who, rather than wait for danger, provoke it.

So, with an almost defiant air, he seated himself beside a young lady dressed in pink *tulle,* and began to laugh and chat with her. He possessed a ready wit, and what is even better, tact; and for a quarter of an hour astonished those around him by his brilliant sallies. Champagne was flowing freely; and he drank four or five glasses in quick succession. Was he really conscious of what he was doing and saying? He subsequently declared that he was not, that he acted under the influence of a sort of hallucination similar to that produced by the inhalation of carbonic gas.

However, the guests did not linger long at the supper-table. "Let us go back!" cried the old gentleman, who had insisted upon the suspension of the game; "we are wasting a deal of precious time here!"

Pascal rose with the others, and in his haste to enter the adjoining room he jostled two men who were talking together near the door. "So it is understood," said one of them.

"Yes, yes, leave it to me; I will act as executioner."

This word sent all Pascal's blood bounding to his heart. "Who is to be executed?" he thought. "I am evidently to be the victim. But what does it all mean?"

Meanwhile the players at the green table had changed places, and Pascal found himself seated not on Ferdinand's right, but directly opposite him, and between two men about his own age—one of them being the person who had announced his intention of acting as executioner. All eyes were fixed upon the unfortunate advocate when it came his turn to deal. He staked two hundred louis, and lost them. There was a slight commotion round the table; and one of the players who had lost most heavily, remarked in an undertone: "Don't look so hard at the gentleman—he won't have any more luck."

As Pascal heard this ironical remark, uttered in a tone which made it as insulting as a blow, a gleam of light darted through his puzzled brain. He suspected at last, what any person less honest than himself would have long before understood. He thought of rising and demanding an apology; but he was stunned, almost overcome by the horrors of his situation. His

ears tingled, and it seemed to him as if the beating of
his heart were suspended.

However the game proceeded; but no one paid any
attention to it. The stakes were insignificant, and loss
or gain drew no exclamation from any one. The attention of the entire party was concentrated on Pascal;
and he, with despair in his heart, followed the movements of the cards, which were passing from hand to
hand, and fast approaching him again. When they
reached him the silence became breathless, menacing,
even sinister. The ladies, and the guests who were not
playing, approached and leaned over the table in evident anxiety. "My God!" thought Pascal, "my God,
if I can only lose!"

He was as pale as death; the perspiration trickled
down from his hair upon his temples, and his hands
trembled so much that he could scarcely hold the cards.
"I will stake four thousand francs," he faltered.

"I take your bet," answered a voice.

Alas! the unfortunate fellow's wish was not grati-
fied; he won. Then in the midst of the wildest
confusion, he exclaimed: "Here are eight thousand
francs!"

"Taken!"

But as he began to deal the cards, his neighbor
sprang up, seized him roughly by the hands and cried:
"This time I'm sure of it—you are a thief!"

With a bound, Pascal was on his feet. While his
peril had been vague and undetermined, his energy had
been paralyzed. But it was restored to him intact when
his danger declared itself in all its horror. He pushed
away the man who had caught his hands, with such
violence that he sent him reeling under a sofa; then
he stepped back and surveyed the excited throng with

an air of menace and defiance. Useless! Seven or eight players sprang upon him and overpowered him, as if he had been the vilest criminal.

Meanwhile, the executioner, as he had styled himself, had risen to his feet with his cravat untied, and his clothes in wild disorder. "Yes," he said, addressing Pascal, "you are a thief! I saw you slip other cards among those which were handed to you."

"Wretch!" gasped Pascal.

"I saw you—and I am going to prove it." So saying he turned to the mistress of the house, who had dropped into an arm-chair, and imperiously asked, "How many packs have we used?"

"Five."

"Then there ought to be two hundred and sixty cards upon the table."

Thereupon he counted them slowly and with particular care, and he found no fewer than three hundred and seven. "Well, scoundrel!" he cried; "are you still bold enough to deny it?"

Pascal had no desire to deny it. He knew that words would weigh as nothing against this material, tangible, incontrovertible proof. Forty-seven cards had been fraudulently inserted among the others. Certainly not by him! But by whom? Still he, alone, had been the gainer through the deception.

"You see that the coward will not even defend himself!" exclaimed one of the women.

He did not deign to turn his head. What did the insult matter to him? He knew himself to be innocent, and yet he felt that he was sinking to the lowest depths of infamy—he beheld himself disgraced, branded, ruined. And realizing that he must meet facts with facts, he besought God to grant him an idea, an inspiration, that would unmask the real culprit.

But another person came to his aid. With a boldness which no one would have expected on his part, M. de Coralth placed himself in front of Pascal, and in a voice which betokened more indignation than sorrow, he exclaimed: "This is a terrible mistake, gentlemen. Pascal Ferailleur is my friend; and his past vouches for his present. Go to the Palais de Justice, and make inquiries respecting his character there. They will tell you how utterly impossible it is that this man can be guilty of the ignoble act he is accused of."

No one made any reply. In the opinion of all his listeners, Ferdinand was simply fulfilling a duty which it would have been difficult for him to escape. The old gentleman who had decided the suspension and the resumption of the game, gave audible expression to the prevailing sentiment of the party. He was a portly man, who puffed like a porpoise when he talked, and whom his companions called the baron. "Your words do you honor—really do you honor," he said, addressing Ferdinand—" and no possible blame can attach to you. That your friend is not an honest man is no fault of yours. There is no outward sign to distinguish scoundrels."

Pascal had so far not opened his lips. After struggling for a moment in the hands of his captors, he now stood perfectly motionless, glancing furiously around him as if hoping to discover the coward who had prepared the trap into which he had fallen. For he felt certain that he was the victim of some atrocious conspiracy, though it was impossible for him to divine what motive had actuated his enemies. Suddenly those who were holding him felt him tremble. He raised his head; he fancied he could detect a ray of hope. " Shall I be allowed to speak in my own defence? " he asked.

" Speak! "

He tried to free himself; but those beside him would not relax their hold, so he desisted, and then, in a voice husky with emotion, he exclaimed: " I am innocent! I am the victim of an infamous plot. Who the author of it is I do not know. But there is some one here who must know." Angry exclamations and sneering laughs interrupted him. " Would you condemn me unheard? " he resumed, raising his voice. " Listen to me. About an hour ago, while you were at supper, Madame d'Argelès almost threw herself at my feet as she entreated me to leave this house. Her agitation astonished me. Now I understand it."

The gentleman known as the baron turned toward Madame d'Argelès : " Is what this man says true? "

She was greatly agitated, but she answered: " Yes."

" Why were you so anxious for him to go? "

" I don't know—a presentiment—it seemed to me that something was going to happen."

The least observant of the party could not fail to notice Madame d'Argelès's hesitation and confusion; but even the shrewdest were deceived. They supposed that she had seen the act committed, and had tried to induce the culprit to make his escape, in order to avoid a scandal.

Pascal saw he could expect no assistance from this source. " M. de Coralth could assure you," he began.

" Oh, enough of that," interrupted a player. " I myself heard M. de Coralth do his best to persuade you not to play."

So the unfortunate fellow's last and only hope had vanished. Still he made a supreme effort, and addressing Madame d'Argelès: "Madame," he said, in a voice trembling with anguish, "I entreat you, tell what you know. Will you allow an honorable man to be ruined before your very eyes? Will you abandon an innocent man whom you could save by a single word?" But she remained silent; and Pascal staggered as if some one had dealt him a terrible blow. "It is all over!" he muttered.

No one heard him; everybody was listening to the baron, who seemed to be very much put out. "We are wasting precious time with all this," said he. "We should have made at least five rounds while this absurd scene has been going on. We must put an end to it. What are you going to do with this fellow? I am in favor of sending for a commissary of police."

Such was not at all the opinion of the majority of the guests. Four or five of the ladies took flight at the bare suggestion and several men—the most aristocratic of the company—became angry at once. "Are you mad?" said one of them. "Do you want to see us all summoned as witnesses? You have probably forgotten that Garcia affair, and that rumpus at Jenny Fancy's house. A fine thing it would be to see, no one knows how many great names mixed up with those of sharpers and notorious women!"

Naturally of a florid complexion, the baron's face now became scarlet. "So it's fear of scandal that deters you! Zounds, sir! a man's courage should equal his vices. Look at me."

Celebrated for his income of eight hundred thousand francs a year, for his estates in Burgundy, for his passion for gaming, his horses, and his cook, the baron wielded a mighty influence. Still, on this occasion he did not carry the day, for it was decided that the

" sharper " should be allowed to depart unmolested.
" Make him at least return the money," growled a
loser; " compel him to disgorge."

" His winnings are there upon the table."

" Don't believe it," cried the baron. " All these
scoundrels have secret pockets in which they stow away
their plunder. Search him by all means."

" That's it—search him ! "

Crushed by this unexpected, undeserved and incom-
prehensible misfortune, Pascal had almost yielded to
his fate. But the shameful cry : " Search him ! " kindled
terrible wrath in his brain. He shook off his assail-
ants as a lion shakes off the hounds that have attacked
him, and, reaching the fireplace with a single bound,
he snatched up a heavy bronze candelabrum and brandished it in the air, crying : " The first who approaches
is a dead man ! "

He was ready to strike, there was no doubt about it ;
and such a weapon in the hands of a determined man,
becomes positively terrible. The danger seemed so
great and so certain that his enemies paused—each
encouraging his neighbor with his glance ; but no one
was inclined to engage in this struggle, by which the
victor would merely gain a few bank-notes. " Stand
back, and allow me to retire ? " said Pascal, imperiously.
They still hesitated ; but finally made way. And, formidable in his indignation and audacity, he reached the
door of the room unmolested, and disappeared.

This superb outburst of outraged honor, this marvellous energy—succeeding, as it did, the most complete
mental prostration—and these terrible threats, had
proved so prompt and awe-inspiring that no one had
thought of cutting off Pascal's retreat. The guests had
not recovered from their stupor, but were still stand-

ing silent and intimidated when they heard the outer
door close after him.

It was a woman who at last broke the spell. " Ah,
well ! " she exclaimed, in a tone of intense admiration,
" that handsome fellow is level-headed ! "

" He naturally desired to save his plunder ! "

It was the same expression that M. de Coralth had
employed; and which had, perhaps, prevented Pascal
⸶from yielding to Madame d'Argelès's entreaties. Everybody applauded the sentiment—everybody, the baron
excepted. This rich man, whose passions had dragged
him into the vilest dens of Europe, was thoroughly
acquainted with sharpers and scoundrels of every type,
from those who ride in their carriages down to the bare-
footed vagabond. He knew the thief who grovels at
his victim's feet, humbly confessing his crime, the desperate knave who swallows the notes he has stolen, the
abject wretch who bares his back to receive the blows
he deserves, and the rascal who boldly confronts his
accusers and protests his innocence with the indignation of an honest man. But never, in any of
these scoundrels, had the baron seen the proud, stead-
fast glance with which this man had awed his accusers.

With this thought uppermost in his mind he drew
the person who had seized Pascal's hands at the card-
table a little aside. " Tell me," said he, " did you
actually see that young man slip the cards into the
pack ? "

" No, not exactly. But you know what we agreed
at supper ? We were sure that he was cheating; and it
was necessary to find some pretext for counting the
cards."

" What if he shouldn't be guilty, after all ? "

"Who else could be guilty then? He was the only winner."

To this terrible argument—the same which had silenced Pascal—the baron made no reply. Indeed his intervention became necessary elsewhere, for the other guests were beginning to talk loudly and excitedly around the pile of gold and bank-notes which Pascal had left on the table. They had counted it, and found it to amount to the sum of thirty-six thousand three hundred and twenty francs; and it was the question of dividing it properly among the losers which was causing all this uproar. Among these guests, who belonged to the highest society—among these judges who had so summarily convicted an innocent man, and suggested the searching of a supposed sharper only a moment before—there were several who unblushingly misrepresented their losses. This was undeniable; for on adding the various amounts that were claimed together a grand total of ninety-one thousand francs was reached. Had this man who had just fled taken the difference between the two sums away with him? A difference amounting almost to fifty-five thousand francs? No, this was impossible; the supposition could not be entertained for a moment. However, the discussion might have taken an unfortunate turn, had it not been for the baron. In all matters relating to cards, his word was law. He quietly said, "It is all right;" and they submitted.

Nevertheless, he absolutely refused to take his share of the money; and after the division, rubbing his hands as if he were delighted to see this disagreeable affair concluded, he exclaimed: "It is only six o'clock; we have still time for a few rounds."

But the other guests, pale, disturbed, and secretly

ashamed of themselves, were eager to depart, and in
fact they were already hastening to the cloak-room.
" At least play a game of écarté," cried the baron,
" a simple game of écarté, at twenty louis a point."

But no one listened, and he reluctantly prepared to
follow his departing friends, who bowed to Madame
d'Argelès on the landing, as they filed by. M. de
Coralth, who was among the last to retire, had already
reached the staircase, and descended two or three steps,
when Madame d'Argelès called to him. " Remain,"
said she; " I want to speak with you."

" You will excuse me," he began; " I——"

But she again bade him " remain " in such an im-
perious tone that he dared not resist. He reascended
the stairs, very much after the manner of a man who
is being dragged into a dentist's office, and followed
Madame d'Argelès into a small boudoir at the end of
the gambling-room. As soon as the door was closed
and locked, the mistress of the house turned to her
prisoner. " Now you will explain," said she. " It was
you who brought M. Pascal Ferailleur here."

" Alas! I know only too well that I ought to beg
your forgiveness. However, this affair will cost me
dear myself. It has already embroiled me in a difficulty with that fool of a Rochecote, with whom I shall
have to fight in less than a couple of hours."

" Where did you make his acquaintance? "

" Whose—Rochecote's? "

Madame d'Argelès's sempiternal smile had altogether
disappeared. " I am speaking seriously," said she, with
a threatening ring in her voice. " How did you happen
to become acquainted with M. Ferailleur? "

" That can be very easily explained. Seven or eight
months ago I had need of an advocate's services, and

he was recommended to me. He managed my case very cleverly, and we kept up the acquaintance."

"What is his position?"

M. de Coralth's features wore an expression of exceeding weariness as if he greatly longed to go to sleep. He had indeed installed himself in a large armchair, in a semi-recumbent position. "Upon my word, I don't know," he replied. "Pascal had always seemed to be the most irreproachable man in the world—a man you might call a philosopher! He lives in a retired part of the city, near the Panthéon, with his mother, who is a widow, a very respectable woman, always dressed in black. When she opened the door for me, on the occasion of my first visit, I thought some old family portrait had stepped down from its frame to receive me. I judge them to be in comfortable circumstances. Pascal has the reputation of being a remarkable man, and people supposed he would rise very high in his profession."

"But now he is ruined; his career is finished."

"Certainly! You can be quite sure that by this evening all Paris will know what occurred here last night."

He paused, meeting Madame Argelès's look of withering scorn with a cleverly assumed air of astonishment. "You are a villain! Monsieur de Coralth," she said, indignantly.

"I—and why?"

"Because it was you who slipped those cards, which made M. Ferailleur win, into the pack; I saw you do it! And yielding to my entreaties, the young fellow was about to leave the house when you, intentionally, prevented him from saving himself. Oh! don't deny it."

M. de Coralth rose in the coolest possible manner. "I deny nothing, my dear lady," he replied
"absolutely nothing. You and I understand each
other."

Confounded by his unblushing impudence, Madame
d'Argelès remained speechless for a moment. "You
confess it!" she cried, at last. "You dare to confess
it! Were you not afraid that I might speak and state
what I had seen?"

He shrugged his shoulders. "No one would have
believed you," he exclaimed.

"Yes, I should have been believed, Monsieur de
Coralth, for I could have given proofs. You must have
forgotten that I know you, that your past life is no
secret to me, that I know who you are, and what dishonored name you hide beneath your borrowed title!
I could have told my guests that you are married—that
you have abandoned your wife and child, leaving them
to perish in want and misery—I could have told them
where you obtain the thirty or forty thousand francs
you spend each year. You must have forgotten that
Rose told me everything, Monsieur—Paul!"

She had struck the right place this time, and with
such precision that M. de Coralth turned livid, and
made a furious gesture, as if he were about to fell her
to the ground. "Ah, take care!" he exclaimed; "take
care!"

But his rage speedily subsided, and with his usual
indifferent manner, and in a bantering tone, he said:
"Well, what of that? Do you fancy that the world
doesn't already suspect what you could reveal? People
have suspected me of being even worse than I am.
When you proclaim on the housetops that I am an adventurer, folks will only laugh at you, and I shall be

none the worse for it. A matter that would crush a dozen men like Pascal Ferailleur would not injure me in the least. I am accustomed to it. I must have luxury and enjoyment, everything that is pleasant and beautiful—and to procure all this, I do my very best. It is true that I don't derive my income from my estate in Brie; but I have plenty of money, and that is the essential thing. Besides, it is so difficult to earn a livelihood nowadays, and the love of luxury is so intense that no one knows at night what he may do— or, rather, what he won't do—the next day. And last, but not least, the people who ought to be despised are so numerous that contempt is an impossibility. A Parisian who happened to be so absurdly pretentious as to refuse to shake hands with such of his acquaintances as were not irreproachable characters, might walk for hours on the Boulevards without finding an occasion to take his hands out of his pockets."

M. de Coralth talked well enough, and yet, in point of fact, all this was sheer bravado on his part. He knew better than any one else, on what a frail and uncertain basis his brilliant existence was established. Certainly, society does show great indulgence to people of doubtful reputation. It shuts its eyes and refuses to look or listen. But this is all the more reason why it should be pitiless when a person's guilt is positively established. Thus, although he assumed an air of insolent security, the " viscount " anxiously watched the effect of his words upon Madame d'Argelès. Fortunately for himself, he saw that she was abashed by his cynicism; and so he resumed: " Besides, as our friend, the baron, would say, we are wasting precious time in discussing improbable, and even impossible, suppositions. I was sufficiently well acquainted with

your heart and your intelligence, my dear madame, to
be sure that you would not speak a word to my dis-
paragement."

" Indeed! What prevented me from doing so?"

" *I* did; or perhaps I ought rather to say, your own
good sense, which closed your mouth when Monsieur
Pascal entreated you to speak in his defence. I am
entitled to considerable indulgence, madame, and a
great deal ought to be forgiven me. *My* mother, unfortunately, was an honest woman, who did not furnish
me with the means of gratifying every whim."

Madame d'Argelès recoiled as if a serpent had suddenly crossed her path.

" What do you mean?" she faltered.

" You know as well as I do."

" I don't understand you—explain yourself."

With the impatient gesture of a man who finds himself compelled to answer an idle question, and assum-
ing an air of hypocritical commiseration, he replied:
" Well, since you insist upon it, I know, in Paris—in
the Rue de Helder, to be more exact—a nice young
fellow, whose lot I have often envied. He has wanted
for nothing since the day he came into the world. At
school, he had three times as much money as his richest
playfellow. When his studies were finished, a tutor
was provided—with his pockets full of gold—to conduct this favored youth to Italy, Egypt, and Greece.
He is now studying law; and four times a year, with
unvarying punctuality, he receives a letter from London containing five thousand francs. This is all the
more remarkable, as this young man has neither a
father nor a mother. He is alone in the world with
his income of twenty thousand francs. I have heard
him say, jestingly, that some good fairy must be watch-

ing over him; but I know that he believes himself to
be the illegitimate son of some great English nobleman. Sometimes, when he has drunk a little too much,
he talks of going in search of my lord, his father."

The effect M. de Coralth had created by these words
must have been extremely gratifying to him, for
Madame d'Argelès had fallen back in her chair, almost
fainting. "So, my dear madame," he continued, "if
I ever had any reason to fancy that you intended causing me any trouble, I should go to this charming youth
and say: 'My good fellow, you are strangely deceived.
Your money doesn't come from the treasure-box of an
English peer, but from a small gambling den with
which I am very well acquainted, having often had
occasion to swell its revenues with my franc-pieces.'
And if he mourned his vanished dreams, I should tell
him: 'You are wrong; for, if the great nobleman is
lost, the good fairy remains. She is none other than
your mother, a very worthy person, whose only object
in life is your comfort and advancement.' And if he
doubted my word, I should bring him to his mother's
house some *baccarat* night; and there would be a scene
of recognition worthy of Fargueil's genius."

Any man but M. de Coralth would have had some
compassion, for Madame d'Argelès was evidently suffering agony. "It is as I feared!" she moaned, in a
scarcely audible voice.

However, he heard her. "What!" he exclaimed in
a tone of intense astonishment; "did you really doubt
it? No; I can't believe it; it would be doing injustice
to your intelligence and experience. Are people like
ourselves obliged to talk in order to understand each
other? Should I ever have ventured to do what I have
done, in your house, if I had not known the secret of

your maternal tenderness, delicacy of feeling, and devotion?"

She was weeping; big tears were rolling down her face, tracing a broad furrow through the powder on her cheeks. "He knows everything!" she murmured; "he knows everything!"

"By the merest chance, I assure you. As I don't like folks to meddle with my affairs, I never meddle with theirs. As I have just said, it was entirely the work of chance. One April afternoon I came to invite you to a drive in the Bois. I was ushered into this very room where we are sitting now, and found you writing. I said I would wait until you finished your letter; but some one called you, and you hastily left the room. How it was that I happened to approach your writing-table I cannot explain; but I did approach it, and read your unfinished letter. Upon my word it touched me deeply. I can give no better proof of the truth of my assertion than the fact that I can repeat it, almost word for word, even now. 'DEAR SIR,'— you wrote to your London correspondent—'I send you three thousand francs, in addition to the five thousand for the regular quarterly payment. Forward the money without delay. I fear the poor boy is greatly annoyed by his creditors. Yesterday I had the happiness of seeing him in the Rue de Helder, and I found him looking pale and careworn. When you send him this money, forward at the same time a letter of fatherly advice. It is true, he ought to work and win an honorable position for himself; but think of the dangers and temptation that beset him, alone and friendless, in this corrupt city.' There, my dear lady, your letter ended; but the name and address were given, and it was easy enough to understand it. You remember, perhaps, a little incident that occurred after your return. On perceiving that you had forgotten your letter, you turned pale and glanced at me. 'Have you read it, and do you understand it?' your eyes asked; while mine replied: 'Yes, but I shall be silent.'"

"And I shall be silent too," said Madame d'Argelès. M. de Coralth took her hand and raised it to his lips. "I knew we should understand each other," he remarked, gravely. "I am not bad at heart, believe me; and if I had possessed money of my own, or a mother like you——"

She averted her face, fearing perhaps that M. de Coralth might read her opinion of him in her eyes; but after a short pause she exclaimed beseechingly: "Now that I am your accomplice, let me entreat you to do all you possibly can to prevent last night's affair from being noised abroad."

"Impossible."

"If not for M. Ferailleur's sake, for the sake of his poor widowed mother."

"Pascal must be put out of the way!"

"Why do you say that? Do you hate him so much then? What has he done to you?"

"To me, personally? Nothing—I even feel actual sympathy for him."

Madame d'Argelès was confounded. "What!" she stammered; "it wasn't on your own account that you did this?"

"Why, no."

She sprang to her feet, and quivering with scorn and indignation, cried: "Ah! then the deed is even more infamous—even more cowardly!" But alarmed by the threatening gleam in M. de Coralth's eyes, she went no further.

"A truce to these disagreeable truths," said he, coldly. "If we expressed our opinions of each other without reserve, in this world, we should soon come to hard words. Do you think I acted for my own pleasure? Suppose some one had seen me when I slipped the cards into the pack. If that had happened, *I* should have been ruined."

"And you think that no one suspects you?"

"No one. I lost more than a hundred louis myself. If Pascal belonged to our set, people might investigate the matter, perhaps; but to-morrow it will be forgotten."

"And will he have no suspicions?"

"He will have no proofs to offer, in any case."

Madame d'Argelès seemed to resign herself to the inevitable. "I hope you will, at least, tell me on whose behalf you acted," she remarked.

"Impossible," replied M. de Coralth. And, consulting his watch, he added, "But I am forgetting myself; I am forgetting that that idiot of a Rochecote is waiting for a sword-thrust. So go to sleep, my dear lady, and —till we meet again."

She accompanied him so far as the landing. "It is quite certain that he is hastening to the house of M. Ferailleur's enemy," she thought. And, calling her confidential servant, "Quick, Job," she said; "follow M. de Coralth. I want to know where he is going. And, above all, take care that he doesn't see you."

V.

IF through the length and breadth of Paris there is a really quiet, peaceful street, a refuge for the thoughtfully inclined, it is surely the broad Rue d'Ulm, which starts from the Place du Panthéon, and finishes abruptly at the Rue des Feuillantines. The shops are unassuming, and so few that one can easily count them. There is a wine-shop on the left-hand side, at the corner of the Rue de la Vieille-Estrapade; then a little toy-shop, then a washerwoman's and then a bookbinder's establishment; while on the right-hand you will find the office of the *Bulletin,* with a locksmith's, a fruiterer's, and a baker's—that is all. Along the rest of the street run several spacious buildings, somewhat austere in appearance, though some of them are surrounded by large gardens. Here stands the Convent of the Sisters of the Cross, with the House of Our Lady of Adoration; while further on, near the Rue des Feuillantines, you find the Normal School, with the office of the General Omnibus Company hard by. At day-time you mostly meet grave and thoughtful faces in the street: priests, *savants,* professors, and clerks employed in the adjacent public libraries. The only stir is round about the omnibus office; and if occasional bursts of laughter are heard they are sure to come from the Normal School. After nightfall, a person might suppose himself to be at least a hundred leagues from the Boulevard Montmartre and the Opera-House, in some quiet old provincial town, at Poitiers, for instance. And it is only on listening attentively that you can catch even a faint echo of the tumult of Paris.

It was in this street—"out of the world," as M. de Coralth expressed it—that Pascal Ferailleur resided with his mother. They occupied a second floor, a pretty suite of five rooms, looking out upon a garden. Their rent was high. Indeed, they paid fourteen hundred francs a year. But this was a burden which Pascal's profession imposed upon him; for he, of course, required a private office and a little waiting-room for his clients. With this exception, the mother and son led a straightened, simple life. Their only servant was a woman who came at seven o'clock to do the heavy work, went home again at twelve, and did not return again until the evening, to serve dinner. Madame Ferailleur attended to everything, not blushing in the least when she was compelled to open the door for some client. Besides, she could do this without the least risk of encountering disrespect, so imposing and dignified were her manners and her person.

M. de Coralth had shown excellent judgment when he compared her to a family portrait. She was, in fact, exactly the person a painter would select to represent some old burgher's wife—a chaste and loving spouse, a devoted mother, an incomparable housewife—in one phrase, the faithful guardian of her husband's domestic happiness. She had just passed her fiftieth birthday, and looked fully her age. She had suffered. A close observer would have detected traces of weeping about her wrinkled eyelids; and the twinge of her lips was expressive of cruel anguish, heroically endured. Still, she was not severe, nor even too sedate; and the few friends who visited her were often really astonished at her wit. Besides, she was one of those women who have no history, and who find happiness in what others would call duty. Her life could be summed up in a single sentence: she had loved; she had mourned.

The daughter of a petty clerk in one of the government departments, and merely dowered with a modest portion of three thousand francs, she had married a young man as poor as herself, but intelligent and industrious, whom she loved, and who adored her. This young man on marrying had sworn that he would make a fortune; not that he cared for money for himself, but he wished to provide his idol with every luxury. His love, enhancing his energy, no doubt hastened his success. Attached as a chemist to a large manufacturing establishment, his services soon became so invaluable to his employers that they gave him a considerable interest in the business. His name even obtained an honorable place among modern inventors; and we are indebted to him for the discovery of one of those brilliant colors that are extracted from common coal. At the end of ten years he had become a man of means. He loved his wife as fondly as on the day of their marriage, and he had a son—Pascal.

Unfortunate fellow! One day, in the full sunshine of happiness and success, while he was engaged in a series of experiments for the purpose of obtaining a durable, and at the same time perfectly harmless, green, the chemicals exploded, smashing the mortar which he held, and wounding him horribly about the head and chest. A fortnight later he died, apparently calm, but in reality a prey to bitter regrets. It was a terrible blow for his poor wife, and the thought of her son alone reconciled her to life. Pascal was now everything to her—her present and her future; and she solemnly vowed that she would make a noble man of him. But, alas! misfortunes never come singly. One

of her husband's friends, who acted as administrator
to the estate, took a contemptible advantage of her in-
experience. She went to sleep one night possessing an
income of fifteen thousand francs, but she awoke to
find herself ruined—so completely ruined that she did
not know where to obtain her dinner for that same
evening. Had she been alone in the world, she would
not have grieved much over the catastrophe, but she
was sadly affected by the thought that her son's future
was, perhaps, irrevocably blighted, and that, in any
case, this disaster would condemn him to enter
life through the cramped and gloomy portals of
poverty.

However, Madame Ferailleur was of too courageous
and too proud a nature not to meet this danger with
virile energy. She wasted no time in useless lamentations.
She determined to repair the harm as far as it was in
her power to repair it, resolving that her son's studies
at the college of Louis-the-Great should not be interrupted, even if she had to labor with her own hands.
And when she spoke of manual toil, it was no wild,
unmeaning exaggeration born of sorrow and a passing
flash of courage. She found employment as a day-
servant and in sewing for large shops, until she at
last obtained a situation as clerk in the establishment
where her husband had been a partner. To obtain this
she was obliged to acquire a knowledge of bookkeep-
ing, but she was amply repaid for her trouble; for the
situation was worth eighteen hundred francs a year,
besides food and lodging. Then only did her efforts
momentarily abate; she felt that her arduous task was
drawing to a happy close. Pascal's expenses at school
amounted to about nine hundred francs a year; she did
not spend more than one hundred on herself; and thus

she was able to save nearly eight hundred francs a
year.

It must be admitted that she was admirably seconded
in her efforts by her son. Pascal was only twelve years
old when his mother said to him: " I have ruined you,
my son. Nothing remains of the fortune which your
father accumulated by dint of toil and self-sacrifice.
You will be obliged to rely upon yourself, my boy.
God grant that in years to come you will not reproach
me for my imprudence."

The child did not throw himself into her arms, but
holding his head proudly erect, he answered: " I shall
love you even more, dear mother, if that be possible.
As for the fortune which my father left you, I will
restore it to you again. I am no longer a school-boy,
I am a man—as you shall see."

One could not fail to perceive that he had taken a
solemn vow. Although he possessed a remarkable
mind, and the power of acquiring knowledge rapidly,
he had, so far, worked indifferently, and then only
by fits and starts, whenever examination time drew
near. But from that day forward he did not lose
a moment. His remarks, which were at once comical
and touching, were those of the head of a family, deeply
impressed by a sense of his own responsibility. " You
see," he said to his companions, who were astonished
at his sudden thirst for knowledge, " I can't afford to
wear out my breeches on the college forms, now that
my poor mother has to pay for them with her work."

His good-humor was not in the least impaired by his
resolve not to spend a single penny of his pocket
money. With a tact unusual at his age, or indeed at
any other, he bore his misfortunes simply and proudly,
without any of the servile humility or sullen envy

which so often accompanies poverty. For three years
in succession the highest prizes at the competitions re-
warded him for his efforts; but these successes, far
from elating him unduly, seemed to afford him but
little satisfaction. "This is only glory," he thought;
and his great ambition was to support himself.

He was soon able to do so, thanks to the kindness
of the head-master, who offered him his tuition gratis
if he would assist in superintending some of the lower
classes. Thus one day when Madame Ferailleur pre-
sented herself as usual to make her quarterly payment,
the steward replied: "You owe us nothing, madame;
everything has been paid by your son."

She almost fainted; after bearing adversity so bravely, this happiness proved too much for her. She could
scarcely believe it. A long explanation was necessary
to convince her of the truth, and then big tears, tears
of joy this time, gushed from her eyes.

In this way, Pascal Ferailleur paid all the expenses
of his education until he had won his degree, arming
himself so as to resist the trials that awaited him, and
giving abundant proof of energy and ability. He
wished to be a lawyer; and the law, he was forced to
admit, is a profession which is almost beyond the reach
of penniless young men. But there are no insurmount-
able obstacles for those whose hearts are really set on
an object. On the very day that Pascal inscribed his
name as a student at the law school, he entered an
advocate's office as a clerk. His duties, which were
extremely tiresome at first, had the two-fold advantage
of familiarizing him with the forms of legal procedure.
and of furnishing him with the means of prosecuting
his studies. After he had been in the office six months,
his employer agreed to pay him eight hundred francs a

year, which were increased to fifteen hundred at the end of the second twelvemonth. In three years, when he had passed his final examination qualifying him to practise, his patron raised him to the position of head-clerk, with a salary of three thousand francs, which Pascal was moreover able to increase considerably by drawing up documents for busy attorneys, and assisting them in the preparation of their least important cases.

It was certainly something wonderful to have achieved such a result in so short a time; but the most difficult part of his task had still to be accomplished. It was a perilous undertaking to abandon an assured position, to cast a certainty aside for the chances of life at the bar. It was a grave step—so grave, indeed, that Pascal hesitated for a long time. He was threatened with the danger that always threatens subordinates who are useful to their superiors. He felt that his employer, who was in the habit of relieving himself of his heaviest duties by intrusting them to him, would not be likely to forgive him for leaving. And on starting on his own account, he could ill afford to dispense with this lawyer's good-will. The patronage that could scarcely fail to follow him from an office where he had served for four years was the most substantial basis of his calculations for the future. Eventually he succeeded to his satisfaction, though not without some difficulty, and only by employing that supreme *finesse* which consists in absolute frankness.

Before his office had been open a fortnight, he had seven or eight briefs waiting their turn upon his desk, and his first efforts were such as win the approving smile of old judges, and draw from them the prediction: "That young man will rise in his profession."

He had not desired to make any display of his knowledge or talent, but merely to win the cases confided to him; and, unlike many beginners, he evinced no inclination to shine at his clients' expense. Rare modesty, and it served him well. His first ten months of practice brought him about eight thousand francs, absorbed in part by the expense attaching to a suitable office. The second year his fees increased by about one-half, and, feeling that his position was now assured, he insisted that his mother should resign her clerkship. He proved to her what was indeed the truth—that by superintending his establishment, she would save more than she made in her present position.

From that time the mother and the son had good reason to believe that their heroic energy had conquered fate. Clients became so numerous that Pascal found it necessary to draw nearer the business centre, and his rent was consequently doubled; but the income he derived from his profession increased so rapidly that he soon had twelve thousand francs safely invested as a resource against any emergency. Madame Ferailleur now laid aside the mourning she had worn since her husband's death. She felt that she owed it to Pascal; and, besides, after believing there was no more happiness left for her on earth, her heart rejoiced at her son's success.

Pascal was thus on the high-road to fame, when a complication in M. Ferdinand de Coralth's affairs brought that young nobleman to his office. The trouble arose from a little stock exchange operation which M. Ferdinand had engaged in—an affair which savored a trifle of knavery. It was strange, but Pascal rather took a liking to M. de Coralth. The honest worker felt interested in this dashing adventurer; he was almost dazzled by his brilliant vices, his wit, his hardihood, conceit, marvellous assurance, and careless impudence; and he studied this specimen of the Parisian flora with no little curiosity. M. de Coralth certainly did not confide the secret of his life and his resources to Pascal; but the latter's intelligence should have told him to distrust a man who treated the requirements of morality even more than cavalierly, and who had infinitely more wants than scruples. However, the young advocate seemed to have no suspicions; they exchanged visits occasionally, and it was Pascal himself who one day requested the viscount to take him to one of those "Reunions in High Life" which the newspapers describe in such glowing terms.

Madame Ferailleur was playing a game of whist with a party of old friends, according to her custom every Thursday evening, when M. de Coralth called to invite the young advocate to accompany him to Madame d'Argelès's reception. Pascal considered his friend's invitation exceedingly well timed. He dressed himself with more than ordinary care, and, as usual before going out, he approached his mother to kiss her and wish her good-bye. "How fine you are!" she said, smiling.

"I am going to a soirée, my dear mother," he replied; "and it is probable that I shall not return until very late. So don't wait for me, I beg of you; promise me to go to bed at your usual hour."

"Have you the night-key?"

"Yes."

"Very well, then; I will not wait for you. When you come in you will find your candle and some matches on the buffet in the ante-room. And wrap yourself up well, for it is very cold." Then raising her forehead to her son's lips, she gayly added: "A pleasant evening to you, my boy!"

Faithful to her promise, Madame Ferailleur retired at the usual hour; but she could not sleep. She certainly had no cause for anxiety, and yet the thought that her son was not at home filled her heart with vague misgivings such as she had never previously felt under similar circumstances. Possibly it was because she did not know where Pascal was going. Possibly M. de Coralth was the cause of her strange disquietude, for she utterly disliked the viscount. Her woman's instinct warned her that there was something unwholesome about this young man's peculiar handsomeness, and that it was not safe to trust to his professions of friendship. At all events, she lay awake and heard the clock of the neighboring Normal School strike each successive hour—two, three, and four. "How late Pascal stays," she said to herself.

And suddenly a fear more poignant even than her presentiments darted through her mind. She sprang out of bed and rushed to the window. She fancied she had heard a terrible cry of distress in the deserted street. At that very moment, the insulting word "thief" was being hurled in her son's face. But the street was silent, and deciding that she had been mistaken, she went back to bed laughing at herself for her fears; and at last she fell asleep. But judge of her terror in the morning when, on rising to let the servant in, she saw Pascal's candle still standing on the buffet. Was it possible that he had not returned? She hastened to his room—he was not there. And it was nearly eight o'clock.

This was the first time that Pascal had spent a night from home without warning his mother in advance;

and such an act on the part of a man of his character
was sufficient proof that something extraordinary had
occurred. In an instant all the dangers that lurk in
Paris after nightfall flashed through her mind. She
remembered all the stories she had read of men decoyed
into dark corners, of men stabbed at the turn of some
deserted street, or thrown into the Seine while crossing
one of the bridges. What should she do? Her first
impulse was to run to the Commissary of Police's office
or to the house of Pascal's friend; but on the other
hand, she dared not go out, for fear he might return
in her absence. Thus, in an agony of suspense, she
waited—counting the seconds by the quick throbbings
of her temples, and straining her ears to catch the
slightest sound.

At last, about half-past eight o'clock, she heard a
heavy, uncertain footfall on the stairs. She flew to the
door and beheld her son. His clothes were torn and
disordered; his cravat was missing, he wore no overcoat, and he was bareheaded. He looked very
pale, and his teeth were chattering. His eyes stared
vacantly, and his features had an almost idiotic expression. "Pascal, what has happened to you?" she
asked.

He trembled from head to foot as the sound of her
voice suddenly roused him from his stupor. "Nothing,"
he stammered; "nothing at all." And as his mother
pressed him with questions, he pushed her gently aside
and went on to his room.

"Poor child!" murmured Madame Ferailleur, at
once grieved and reassured; "and he is always so
temperate. Some one must have forced him to drink."

She was entirely wrong in her surmise, and yet
Pascal's sensations were exactly like those of an in-